Praise for Sweetgirl

"*Sweetgirl* works on so many levels, it's difficult to know how to classify it. As a thriller, it's pretty much perfect; Mulhauser doesn't waste a single word, and the novel is calculated down to the sentence. He builds suspense expertly, and the action scenes are (at one point, quite literally) explosive. But there's so much more going on. Mulhauser treats his characters with a stunning sense of compassion. . . . Mixing humor and tragedy is always a difficult balancing act, particularly in a novel dealing with drug addiction, broken families and violence, and the fact that Mulhauser pulls it off so brilliantly in a debut novel is something like a miracle. *Sweetgirl* is hilarious, heartbreaking and true, a major accomplishment from an author who looks certain to have an impressive career ahead of him." —NPR

"You can't help but smile at this disarmingly original novel. . . . Travis Mulhauser traverses a wobbling slack line across a moral crevasse that few of us will experience. Yet there's a devastating credibility to the events he creates." —*Star Tribune* (Minneapolis)

"Travis Mulhauser delivers the perfect balance of humor and heartache in this masterful debut novel about family, self-reliance, and atonement. When 16-year-old Percy James ventures out in a fierce Michigan snow storm in hopes of rescuing her mother whom she suspects is strung out in the local meth dealer's farmhouse, instead she finds a baby in desperate need of a doctor. In order to save both the baby and herself, Percy confronts the dark and misunderstood members of Cutler County's underbelly society: a drug kingpin's nephew, his gun-wielding, whiskey-drinking cronies, and an unrelenting winter blizzard. What she finds along the way is strength beyond measure, a friend more loyal than family, and a long-shot's chance for hope. This book is as wise as it is suspenseful, as funny as it is tragic. A novel written with guts, grit, and grace, *Sweetgirl* is the book you want to keep you company on a cold winter's night." —*Ploughshares*

"Smart, taut, and believable writing" — *St. Louis Post-Dispatch*

"Though the story takes place in a chaotic Michigan blizzard, fans of Ozark-based grit lit will feel right at home in Travis Mulhauser's gorgeous, lyrical *Sweetgirl*. . . . With characters that toe the line between doom and hope, *Sweetgirl* delivers compelling, emotional resonance." —Paste Magazine

The writing is gorgeous and the stakes rise steadily from the moment Percy first sets out, making this slim novel surprisingly vicious and taut. —Bookriot.com

"Here's one due in February that's so good that I read a few paragraphs aloud to my podiatrist as he removed a toenail. Honest. It's *Sweetgirl*, by Travis Mulhauser of Durham. Though meth and drugs infest almost every page, this debut novel is chillingly lyrical and filled with a love so raw and fierce it takes your breath." —*Charlotte Observer*

"Mulhauser has created a suspenseful tale of sadness and redemption." —*Herald-Sun* (Durham, NC)

"*Sweetgirl* is a gritty, compelling novel of a world where even a sixteen-year-old must confront what Edith Wharton called 'the hard considerations of the poor.' Mulhauser depicts his people and their landscape with uncompromising fidelity." —Ron Rash

"Travis Mulhauser's *Sweetgirl* is a compulsively readable novel—no doubt about it—finish the first chapter and you will be hooked, I guarantee. This book is violent, dark, and impressively redemptive. Villains are haunted by their innocent victims and somehow discover grace. Heroes are flawed, fallible, and reek of whiskey and regret. And perhaps at the center of Mulhauser's novel is an unlikely character who never speaks a word, never takes a step, but propels the entire story along like a runaway eighteen-wheeler. *Sweetgirl* is an upper-Midwestern homage to great American quest novels like *True Grit* and *Winter's Bone*. It is a truly memorable and remarkable read."

—Nickolas Butler, internationally bestselling author of
Shotgun Lovesongs and *Beneath the Bonfire*

"Travis Mulhauser's *Sweetgirl* is a riveting novel about a bunch of drug addicts and drug dealers and boozers and quasi-orphans and quasi-parents dealing with the prospect of a missing baby girl during a massive snowstorm in northern Michigan. This sounds grim, and it can be grim, but this book is also far, far funnier than it has any right to be. If you're a fan of Charles Portis and Denis Johnson—and if you're not, you should be—then this is book is exactly what you've been wanting, what you've been waiting for."

—Brock Clarke, author of *The Happiest People in the World*

"In its dark and deadpan hilarity, *Sweetgirl* reminded me of other great chroniclers of the criminal element found in our upper Midwest—Tom Drury, Jim Harrison, the Coen Brothers in *Fargo*. But Mulhauser's Cutler County, a place of numbered days and last chances, is a part of that country we've not seen before. Nor have we heard it described in a voice like Percy James's, filled with true wit, cunning, and the unwanted wisdom of a child denied a childhood. This novel comes on like the blizzard at its center, and leaves you dazzled and dazed not only by how much Travis Mulhauser knows, but how deeply he cares." —Michael Parker, author of *All I Have in This World*

Sweetgirl

ALSO BY TRAVIS MULHAUSER

Greetings from Cutler County: A Novella and Stories

Sweetgirl

Travis Mulhauser

ecco
An Imprint of HarperCollinsPublishers

This book is a work of fiction. The characters, incidents, and dialogue are drawn from the author's imagination and are not to be construed as real. Any resemblance to actual events or persons, living or dead, is entirely coincidental.

SWEETGIRL. Copyright © 2016 by Travis Mulhauser. All rights reserved. Printed in the United States of America. No part of this book may be used or reproduced in any manner whatsoever without written permission except in the case of brief quotations embodied in critical articles and reviews. For information address HarperCollins Publishers, 195 Broadway, New York, NY 10007.

HarperCollins books may be purchased for educational, business, or sales promotional use. For information please e-mail the Special Markets Department at SPsales@harpercollins.com.

A hardcover edition of this book was published in 2016 by Ecco, an imprint of HarperCollins Publishers.

FIRST ECCO PAPERBACK EDITION PUBLISHED 2016.

Designed by Sunil Manchikanti
Title page photograph: Yankee Springs State Parks, Michigan © Dean Pennala / Shutterstock, Inc.

Library of Congress Cataloging-in-Publication Data has been applied for.

ISBN 978-0-06-240083-3

16 17 18 19 20   OV/RRD   10 9 8 7 6 5 4 3 2 1

for Cassy

Acknowledgments

Leo and Edie Lou, who are my beating hearts and who taught me a lot about everything. Susan Ramer, for being spectacular. My editor, Megan Lynch, for her talent, vision, and guiding hand. And everybody at Ecco who has done so much for this book. Søren Palmer, for all the rides and the readings. Jon Baker, for all the answered questions. The Sustainable Arts Foundation, for their incredible generosity. For their readings and many areas of expertise: Fred Mulhauser, Whitney Mulhauser, Cassy Stubbs, Laura Waldrep and Matt Norcross. For their endless support, Joanna Kolodziej and Kyler Mulhauser. And for all sorts of stuff, this list of stellar human beings: Pamela Kolodziej, Emily Dings, the Gillmors, the Reddings, Niels Lunsgaard, Matt Gallagher, Gill Pulley, Robert Sorrenti, Rebo Sullivan, Susan Miller-Cochran, Michael Parker, Terry Kennedy, the Aarons, John and Terri Lee, and Louise Deaton.

Chapter One

Nine days after Mama disappeared I heard she was throwing down with Shelton Potter. Gentry said she was off on a bad one and wandering around the farmhouse like a goddamn ghost.

Mama bought her booze at Night Moves, where Gentry worked the counter, and he stopped by to tell me he saw her at Shelton's while he was out there delivering a keg.

"When?" I said.

"Last night," he said. "I've been meaning to come by."

The only thing that surprised me was my own surprise. As many times as Carletta let me down I still felt all gut-punched and woozy, like it was the first time she forgot to pick me up from school.

"She didn't even recognize me," he said. "It was like she looked right through me."

Gentry took a puff of his clove and pulled his knit hat down over his ears. He had seven years on me but we were friends. He sold me cigarettes at the store even though I only turned sixteen that summer and I was always supportive when he had some drama with a boyfriend.

He looked at me with sad eyes. He said he could come in if I felt like talking, but I didn't see the point. Gentry was a good listener and there was plenty I could say about Mama, but none of it was going to bring her home.

I grabbed my hoodie off the hook, thanked Gentry for looking out, and made for the pickup. He called after me from the porch, but I kept going.

It was late and cold and I was bone tired. I work at Pickering's Furniture, and I'd stripped and sanded two small tables and a chest of drawers that night. I didn't lock the shed until after eight, but what was I supposed to do? Stretch out on the couch like everything was copacetic?

No, I started the truck instead. I cranked the heat and looked out at the falling snow. There was a norther on the way but the apocalypse itself wouldn't stop Mama if she was already in orbit—so I gunned it down Clark Street and set out for the north hills like a solid-gold fool.

Our block was all beat-down rentals and busted-up fence, but the digs were even worse when I hit Detroit Street, where the Mexicans stayed. Carletta called it the barrio and liked to cluck her tongue when we rolled by those crumbling-down row houses. She liked to say she didn't understand how some people lived.

I never bothered to point out that we were just a few blocks away, in a one-bedroom, and that I didn't know whether to say I slept in the living room or the kitchen because the couch was technically in both. The irony would have been lost on Mama, who always said we had an "open floor plan"—like we lived in some magazine house where everything was spread out nice and all the fabric matched the throw pillows. Like we put out bowls of decorative fruit, just because.

It's not that I minded the couch. I slept like a baby. It was just that Carletta had a way of denying certain realities to make her life seem like more than it was, which was sort of like coping, but was mostly just another way to lie.

Still, I missed her. I missed her and I was tired of my waiting-around, worried-sick life. I was tired of the wondering where she was, and of the constant alarm that gripped my heart like a strangler vine.

So I took Detroit Street to Grove, which led me toward town, where the homes and lives improved considerably. There were the local well-to-do in their big brick houses, and beyond them the shoreline where the real cash was. The downstate and Chicago money put their roots down in sand—their seasonals all perfectly placed along the water for maximum panorama, and not a soul there to enjoy it because it wasn't nice that time of year.

I couldn't blame them. It was the middle of January in Cutler County, Michigan. We're at the northwest tip of the lower peninsula, the top of your left ring finger if you map it by the back of your hand, and unless you go in for the whole Jack London, ends-of-the-earth vibe, why wouldn't you fly off to somewhere else if you could? It was only nine o'clock at night and downtown was already three blocks of black windows behind high banks of snow and there wasn't a single other car in the streets.

I sailed through a blinking red onto 31 North, then took the highway past the old cement plant and the Shoreline Estates trailer park. The wind was hard off the bay and I could see the shape of the north hills in the distance—a jagged, soot-colored line through the snow.

I wished I could stop at Portis Dale's. Portis was the closest thing I had to a father and he had a cabin not a half mile from Shelton's. I'd have much preferred to take him to the farmhouse with me, and would have begged him gladly if I thought there was half a chance he would.

The problem was, Portis quit chasing Carletta years ago and was liable to bind me to a chair for the duration of the winter if I so much as made a whisper about Shelton Potter's. I could hear him clear as day.

"That farmhouse ain't no place for a girl," he would say. "No place for you."

Portis might have been right, but I drove on anyway. I drove despite the broken promises and heartache and all the lying and stealing and flimsy, sorry-as-hell excuses. I ignored my own good sense and the coming storm and exited the highway onto Grain Road and took it along the Three Fingers River.

The road and the river ran a crooked line and halved the hills from top to bottom. To the east was nothing but deep forest and some fishing ponds, while the west was a wide scatter of cabins and trailers connected by two-tracks and snowmobile trails.

The north hills were only five minutes from town, but they might as well have been a hundred miles from those big houses along the bay. The second you turned into the hills it was like somebody flipped a switch. The high trees swallowed the stars and the city lights and there were times it felt like you were dropping. There were spots in the hills where you could see out, clearings that let in some light, but the drive up felt like shooting straight down a mine shaft.

I took the switchbacks and was surprised the radio signal held—Kid Rock going on about fishing walleye while I peered out and looked for my turn.

Grain Road was paved beneath the snow but I'd have to veer off to get to Shelton's. It concerned me some, but the farmhouse wasn't too far off the river and I'd avoid the tangle of two-tracks that run farther west.

My high beams weren't much use against the dark, but I saw the bend where the river hit the big rocks between ice floes and shot white water. The entrance road to Shelton's was at the next break in the pines and I let the old Nissan ease through a fishtail when I took it.

The road was narrow, but there was a stretch a quarter mile in where it swung out and showed the clearing where the farmhouse sat on the edge of Jackson Lake. On a nice day you could spot the color of the front door from that ridge, but in the dark I couldn't see anything beneath me but a big, empty bowl of black.

I came off the ridge and the road tightened as it wound deeper into the trees. I drove until I came to the edge of Shelton's property where a million flagged stakes and tree-nailed signs were marked NO TRESPASS. I didn't give a rat's ass about Shelton Potter's property rights, but I didn't want to go much farther and get pinned in by the snow. I could already feel my tires starting to drop, so I idled the truck and sat inside while I plotted the best course in by foot.

I figured I was a mile from the front door by land. The quickest route would be across the lake, but I hate to walk hardwater in the dark. I knew the ice was likely to hold, but say it didn't? One misstep and I could be in a bad way quick—ice crackling as the splits spread like taproots and opened into breaks.

I would have to hike the rest of the way through the woods, then cross open land to get to the farmhouse. It would be cold and dark and purely miserable, but I'd keep walking until I got there because I didn't have a choice. Carletta had to be got.

I leaned toward the vents and wrapped my arms tight around my chest to pull the heat in. Mama had seen fit to steal my winter coat and gloves the night she disappeared, which meant I would be making the trek in my hoodie and blue jeans. An injustice that might have angered me if I thought it would do any good.

Snow was already piling on the hood of the truck. They cut into the radio with a weather advisory and after the warning sirens came the voice of Lester Hoffstead, northern Michigan's most trusted name in weather. He was in a tizzy over his Doppler radar and its dire predictions and I reached out to punch the power off. No offense to Lester, but I understood it was a damn blizzard coming.

I pushed the door open and felt the cold come over me in a wash. I tightened my hood strings and ran for the cover of the trees.

I moved through the pines at the edge of the property without much problem, but when the woods cleared and I hit the open fields the snow got deep. The wind was hard against me and I had to drop my head low against the gusting. I fisted my hands at my side and walked.

It was the burning kind of cold. A tear had opened in my lip and I put my tongue to it and tasted the salty, pooling blood. There was already a throb and tingle in my toes and the air torched my lungs just to breathe it. I looked back after a minute and could not see the pinewoods or tell the falling snow in the fields from what was wind-thrown.

Shelton lived in the farmhouse, but it was his uncle Rick who owned the north hills. Rick had most everything west of the river, where he rented plots to his cronies and had built himself a spread on top that he faced toward the setting sun. Even Portis was on Rick's land, a holdover from the days when he ran with those idiots.

Rick was raised in the hills and earned his money in cocaine and marijuana, legitimate markets in comparison to Shelton's preference for home-cooked methamphetamines. Rick had long-standing agreements with Cutler law and was a high school football hero to boot. People still bought him drinks on account of some la-de-da record he set against Cheboygan, and every

Christmas he stood on Mitchell Street in a Santa suit and roasted chestnuts for the Kiwanis Club.

Rick Potter was a pillar of the community, while Shelton had done a stint in the Ionia penitentiary and smoked his own cook—a source of considerable tension between the two. People said Shelton was the bad guy, but I didn't like either one on principle. I didn't care to make distinctions between the ways they conducted their criminal lives, but it was Shelton I feared as I walked through the dark.

The drifts finally lowered near the house and there were rutted trails and some hard-packed snow to set my feet in. I could see the farmhouse now, a bluish smudge through my wind-teared eyes, and Carletta's Bonneville parked out back and buried beneath a foot of powder.

I didn't come up the front steps. I flanked the house instead, then hoisted myself over the railing on the far side of the porch. There was a wide, double-hung window along the wall and I crouched beside it and cleared snow with my sleeve.

The living room was low lit, but I could see Shelton's sorry behind through the glass. He was shirtless and laid out on the couch in blue jeans. He had WHITEBOY tattooed on his back—lest he be mistaken for a black albino—and I could see the Old English scrawl along the bony jut of his shoulder. I could see a rash of acne on his back as he faced the center of the room and slept.

The coffee table was cluttered with tinfoil, pipes, and ash, and there was a shotgun leaned against the wall beside it. There was a woman on the floor in blue jeans and a black sweater. Her blond hair was pulled back and I could see the hard line of her jaw and two scrawny arms stretched above her head like she'd been reaching for something. She looked familiar somehow, but I thought it was probably just that she resembled Carletta when she crashed. She was all contorted and trampled-looking and facedown on the floor like some corpse washed up on the beach.

I hurried to the back of the house where steps led to the rear entrance. The wind was deadened some by the pole barn behind me and I could hear the stereo blaring inside. I could hear the thump of bass and a man's voice above guitars. The backdoor opened into the kitchen and I stood there in the cold with my hand against the icy knob.

I had my moment of doubt. Part of me wanted to drop the whole thing right there and hoof it back to the truck. I knew how stupid it was to walk in that back door, but Mama had to be found. There was no guarantee she would survive the storm, assuming she hadn't curled herself into a corner of the farmhouse and died already.

The knob turned in my palm and I stepped inside and was brushed back by the stink. I don't know why I was surprised the place smelled like the circus, but I had to take a minute and stand there with my breath held.

The floor was littered with trash and animal droppings and the stereo rattled empties on the countertop. There was a Maine coon cat curled atop Gentry's keg and it startled me so bad I gasped when I saw it—a frenzy of orange-white fur, licking at its paws all lazy like. I nodded and the cat trailed me with its yellowy eyes.

The man on the stereo sang something about fur pajamas and I took a short breath and crossed the room. I had a small Maglite on my key chain and I followed its tiny beam to a staircase between the kitchen and the living room. I was glad for the music, otherwise I know Shelton Potter could have heard my heart beat out loud.

Check out Mr. Businessman, said the singer.

The stink got worse when I reached the second story and I buried my nose in the crook of my arm and whispered for Carletta. I scanned the floor with my flashlight.

The hall was narrow and unlit. The wallpaper was patterned with roosters and torn in wide strips and beneath the paper I could see the wood framing and feel the cold whistling through.

There was a door on each side of the hall and when I opened the first the stench was like a wall I walked smack into. I jerked at the shoulders and braced myself in the doorframe but couldn't keep from retching. It was the foulest odor I have ever encountered and I knew right off to call it death. I retched a second time and then shone my light.

The dog was lying stiff on the carpet in the center of the room and I cried out when I saw its unmoving, marble eyes. I saw the snout receding toward the collapsed jaw, and the fur that lay puddled where the muscles had gone soft. I backed out of the room and had to keep myself from slamming the door in a rage.

You want to bake your own brain with a bunch of damn Drano, then fine, but leave a helpless animal trapped and starving to death while you did it? I was shaking angry and had a thought like I should go downstairs and suffocate that sonofabitch, Shelton, in his sleep. Or shoot him if the shotty was loaded.

It was the kind of thought you have because you know you won't do anything with it, but it makes you feel better for a second to think that you might. I'm not a killer and even if I was, who was going to take care of Carletta while I rotted in prison for doing the world the good turn of putting out Shelton Potter's lights?

I returned to my search and whispered for Mama. I asked if she was there. There was no reply from the hall, and as I eased the other door open I held in my heart a desperate and wordless prayer about what I would find there.

The room was lit with a single, exposed bulb that flickered and cast a dusty light from the ceiling. There was a flood of cold through an open window along the side wall, and there was snow piling on the sill and the carpet. A mattress lay cockeyed on the floor and between the mattress and a radiator I saw a bassinet. Inside the bassinet was a baby.

The man on the stereo was back to the part about fur pajamas. I didn't know if the song was on repeat, or the singer had felt the need to double back and touch on that particular detail again.

Things fall apart, he went on. *It's scientific.*

I could see the baby was shrieking, but its cries were buried by the wind. The snow blew in sideways, edged across the floor, and dusted the baby's cheeks with frost. The baby's eyes darted in a side-to-side panic as it reached up with trembling hands and searched for something to grasp.

I ran toward it.

Chapter Two

Crisis is a constant when you're a daughter of Carletta James, which prevented me from outright panic at the sight of an abandoned infant in the farmhouse. This is not to say I was unsurprised by the discovery of the bassinet, or the sight of the baby wailing against the wind. Of course these things surprised me, and filled me with a momentary terror—it's just that I could not allow my shock to extend beyond a clipped breath or two. While the particulars of a given calamity may be impossible to predict, while I could never say I expected to find a baby in the bedroom, chaos itself was always confirmation of the dread I carried blood-deep and certain in my bones.

On the side of the bassinet BABY JENNA was written in marker and surrounded by flowers that had been carefully woven between the letters.

"Shh," I whispered, and lifted her out.

Her pajamas were cold and clung sticky and wet at the back. She reeked of shit and the soured tang of spit-up and I felt her little chest heave as she cried. Her cheeks were icy to the touch and I cleared them of snow as I rocked her in my arms. Her chin was collapsed as she sobbed and her eyes scrambled from me to the room and then back. Her hands were curled and she seemed to be both reaching for me and shielding herself against my presence. I kept hushing her. I didn't know what else to do.

Her eyes were greenish gray, the color of the sky edge before a storm, and her black hair shot off in all directions and curled over her ears. I stood with her in the doorway, keeping an eye on the hall and the stairs, and that was when she wrapped a hand around my finger and squeezed.

You see pictures all the time of little babies' hands, and often they are juxtaposed against the much larger grip of an adult. Often these pictures are used by anti-abortion groups or posted on Facebook by self-righteous rich girls with some moralistic message—but I will tell you that there is true power in that little hand. I will tell you it stopped my heart cold when I felt her clutch. I looked down at her and knew I would not be leaving her in that house. I rocked her and whispered until the crying finally quieted and went even in her lungs.

There was a backpack on the floor beside the bassinet and I held her with one hand and rifled through the bag with the other. There was a change of clothes inside, some diapers, a bottle, a canister of powdered formula, and a rattle.

Jenna started to squirm and I unzipped my hoodie and slipped her inside. She was in desperate need of a change, but it wasn't the time or place. I covered everything but her mouth, put the back-pack on over my shoulder, and eased us down the hall.

I held my breath as we passed the dog and watched as Jenna lay perfectly still inside the hoodie. Her eyes were peeled wide open and she looked at me flatly and with what appeared to be the certainty of her trust. The song on the stereo was on repeat. I was sure of it now.

Speak up, the man sang. *I can't hear you.*

There were wet spots on the stairs from where I'd dropped snow, and I looked carefully at each step as we went down. I noted the worn patches of wood and felt the old house settling in the wind. I put a hand flat against the wall to guide us where the steps turned into the landing and hoped we wouldn't be betrayed by a creak in the floorboards.

I would leave out the back and head straight for Portis's place. My truck was just as far away from the farmhouse as the cabin, and all of it uphill. If Shelton or the girl bothered to notice the baby was gone they'd fire up the sleds and the truck and head right for the road I'd come in on. No, the best thing was to go and get Portis. Have him drive us to the hospital in his Ranger.

Potter and the girl hadn't so much as stirred. They were lying exactly as I had found them as I hurried through the kitchen and out the back door into the wind and snow-swirled dark.

My flashlight wasn't much use outside, not after I'd cleared the rutted trails close to the farmhouse and the dark spiraled out and grew deeper. I walked for some time, worrying when Jenna cried, and worrying worse when she didn't. I walked until my legs began to wobble and a sweat had broken on the small of my back. I carried Jenna with both arms and carefully cradled her head.

I had on my combat boots, which I'd bought on a discount at the army-navy store. They were made in Bangladesh and were actually for boys at a military academy, rather than being U.S. Army issue, which the crazy militia man had explained to me as he passed them over the counter like a bag of fruit-rotted garbage. I thought he was trying to shame me into a steeper purchase, but he was right to sneer at my sorry boots. I had my gym socks pulled up around my calves but I could still feel the cold leaking through the eyelets and the tongue.

I pushed through the drifts, but of course the snow found a tiny crease of skin beneath the boot lining and decided to pile up there and rub me raw. And that's the problem with the winter in Cutler County—it's not so much the cold, it's the fact that at some point the ass kicking feels personal.

Even worse, I started to wonder if I was wandering circles through the fields. The farmhouse was only a half mile from Portis's and it felt like too much time had passed since I left Shelton's. I couldn't find the cabin and I couldn't tell one drift of pitch-black snow from the next.

Of course, if Carletta hadn't stopped paying Sprint I would have had my phone with me and I could have checked the time while I called for help. I could have called 911 the second I found Jenna, but Carletta quit paying the bill two weeks before she disappeared and my phone was in a desk drawer at home, right beside my prepaid that was all out of minutes.

I squatted low to the ground to rest and watched my breath trail. The cold was inside me now, like a heaviness in my blood, and I started to worry that I was passing it to Jenna the same way bodies share heat. I'd done a paper on hypothermia once and knew the cold was unpredictable. There was a little girl in Iceland who survived a night in the wilderness at 35 below, while another man had died after just a few hours in temperatures above freezing. I couldn't remember what the point of the paper was though, or if there was something the girl had done to protect herself that the man hadn't.

I might have known better what to do if I'd have been a Girl Scout. I'd always envied those little snots in grade school, with their smart uniforms and badges and altruistic fund-raisers for starving African babies. I'd also envied them their mothers, who all looked like Sandra Bullock and wore Pleiades pants when they came to homeroom to recruit new members. I had badly wanted to join, but I knew they didn't mean me when they asked if anybody was interested in becoming a scout.

Yes, there was surely a world of information I would have had at my disposal had my childhood not been spent caring for Carletta and worrying over Cutler Family Services, wondering when they might finally arrive to take me and my sister, Starr, away for good.

I suppose the Girl Scouts would have known exactly what to do in my very situation, though none of them would ever have occasion to be there in the first place—Sandra Bullock moms not being the type to vanish after trading their daughters' cell service for a few rocks of methamphetamine. Ironies abounded out there in the fields, but I resisted the urge to indulge in their bitterness as I stood up and returned to my march.

What I should have done was walk straight for the river, then turn downstream. That's what the Girl Scouts would have taught me. Go to the river and that will keep you on course. Can't miss a big-ass river. But no, I'd just run out into the dark and hoped I knew where I was going. I'd just taken one step after another and felt vaguely that I was heading in the right direction. I suppose I panicked.

When I saw some light in the far away I worried for a moment that I had simply traced a giant circle back to the farmhouse. I approached with some caution, but then I saw the line of the river behind the cabin. I saw the telltale slant of Portis's roof and heard Wolfdog barking at the wind.

Chapter Three

Portis greeted me like he does all his houseguests—with the barrel end of his rifle. He aimed through a slit cut in the cabin door and demanded I identify myself.

"It's Percy!" I said. "Open up!"

I kept Jenna close and stepped away from Wolfdog. She'd turned her bark on me, but I was more hurt than frightened. I'd known Wolfdog since she was a pup and spent whole days fishing the Three Fingers with her and Portis. I loved Wolfdog and I always thought she loved me back, but she was leaned forward on her front paws and flashing her canines like switchblade knives. She was supposed to be part husky, but she looked all wolf at the moment.

"Hurry," I said. "It's freezing."

"Step back," Portis said, and pushed open the door.

He came out in a T-shirt, gym shorts, and boots. He still had his rifle raised.

"Portis," I said. "It's me."

"Well, shit the bed," he said, and lowered the barrel.

Inside, Portis looked me over with his narrow, searching eyes. He set the rifle down and checked the door latch. He looked at Jenna and tugged at his scraggly, gray-streaked beard. Wolfdog was still barking outside and she leapt at the window and dragged her nails across the glass. Portis reached for a bottle of whiskey on the table and had a pull.

"Is that a fucking baby?" he said.

He had the generator humming. There were Christmas lights strung across the ceiling beams and one of his 1970s bands was on the FM radio, singing about lonely nights.

"That's a fucking baby, isn't it?"

Jenna was fairly calm and now I was the one crying. I could feel the tears stinging the cold tops of my cheeks. It was a baby.

"It's a baby girl," I said, and sniffed.

"Is that your baby girl?"

"What? No!"

"Whose fucking baby is that?"

"I don't know!"

My voice cracked as I raised it in irritation, in outrage at the entire situation. Portis went back to the door and opened the slit. He peered out while Wolfdog barked and batted at the windows.

"What's wrong with Wolfdog?"

"She don't like surprises," he said.

"She's usually so sweet."

"She's got a bad omen."

"What's that mean?"

"She's on edge, goddamnit! She's got a bad feeling in her wolf bones, set her to barking about twenty minutes ago."

"Maybe it's the storm," I said.

"It's supposed to storm in the winter," he said. "I'd probably go with you and that baby as the event of note here. Now, please tell me whose baby that is."

"I just told you, I don't know. Some girl's."

"Some girl?"

"I found her."

"At the farmhouse?"

I shifted Jenna in my arms and stripped off my hoodie. I stood by the woodstove in my T-shirt and blue jeans while Jenna let out a little squawk. I tried to hush her, which seemed preferable to dealing with Portis and his agitations.

"You smoking shit now, Percy?"

"No."

"Don't lie to me."

"I swear," I said.

"So you just wandered up to the farmhouse for no reason? After all the times I've warned you about what goes on up there?"

"Gentry came by," I said. "He saw Mama when he was up there delivering a keg."

"And what are you doing cavorting with the likes of Gentry?"

"He's my friend," I said. "He sells me my cigarettes at the store."

"You're sixteen years old, last I checked."

"You gave me Marlboro Reds when I was twelve!"

"That was to keep you from stealing them."

"What's the difference?"

"It don't even matter," Portis said, and waved his hand. "Just stay the hell away from that Gentry. He's a thirty-year-old man and I can guarantee he's the type that only does a favor cause he's expecting a payback in return. And you know what kind of payback I mean."

"He's twenty-three," I said. "And gay."

"Gay nothing," Portis said. "Gay ain't always what it looks like on the surface."

"Jesus Christ," I said. "You really are a lunatic."

"And just think," he said. "I'm the one you came to for help."

In the firelight, even with his beard in full bloom, I could see the white flecks of scar tissue that covered Portis's face like paint splatters. I could see the left eyelid and where it had grown together at the edge of the socket and left him in a forever squint. He had survived his own run on Shelton's dope, but stuck to drinking now. I suppose it was a slower, more reasonably portioned suffering.

He took another gulp of whiskey and I laid out the facts before he could set in on me again. I told him Mama had gone missing and that her Bonneville was parked out front of Shelton's but that she was not inside. I'd come in the back door and found the baby upstairs while Shelton and the mother were passed out in the living room. I described the bassinet by the open window and how the snow was slanting in. I told him Shelton and the woman hadn't moved an inch and that I was absolutely certain nobody had seen me.

"You're sure about that?" he said.

"Positive," I said. "Nobody saw anything."

Portis turned to the window and frowned at Wolfdog's barking.

"Just a minute," he said, and finally set his whiskey down.

He opened the door and I felt the wind thread through the floorboards as he stepped outside to squat beside Wolfdog. He stroked her neck, hugged her close, then whispered something in her ear and she bounded off and was gone.

Portis knew she was too wound up. Wolfdog would lunge on sight if Shelton Potter showed and that man would not hesitate for a second to put her down. I thought of the dead dog in the farmhouse and felt a shiver slide all the way up my spine.

"I'm sorry," I said, when Portis came back inside. "I saw her there and didn't know what else to do. I just grabbed her."

"Well," he said. "You done something, I guess."

"She seems okay," I said. "Considering."

"She's better off than she was," he said. "Trapped in that farmhouse with Shelton Potter."

"Will you hold her?" I asked. "Just for a minute?"

"I'm not holding any baby," Portis said.

"My arms are going to fall off, Portis. I can't just set her down on the floor."

"I'm not skilled in the area of infant care," he said. "I lack tenderness."

"Please."

"Babies don't like me."

"Everybody likes you."

Portis gulped from his bottle, then wiped the corners of his mouth with his shirtsleeve. He glanced at Jenna and then looked away.

"You better take them clothes off and set them by the woodstove," he said. "I got a blanket you can cover up with. Got some clean woman clothes around here, belonged to a former acquaintance of mine."

"You think he'll come looking?" I said. "Shelton?"

"He'll come looking," he said.

I handed Jenna to Portis and she howled on cue.

"Goddamnit," he said. "I told you."

"You're doing fine," I said. "Just hold her."

"She's small as anything."

"I think she's about six months," I said.

"She's wet."

"We're going to change her and get her fed. I got some formula in the bag if you've got any bottled water. Then we've got to get her someplace safe and warm. I thought you could drive us to the hospital."

"I got water," he said. "But no truck."

"What happened to your truck?"

"Nothing," he said. "It's up the hill."

"How far?" I said.

"Far enough."

"What's it doing up the hill?"

"Sitting, I expect."

"Why is it that the truck is up there and you're down here?"

"There are reasons," he said.

By "reasons" Portis meant he'd driven up the hill to check his traps, gotten too drunk, and wandered around the woods until he forgot what he was doing and came back to the cabin.

"Where's your pickup?" he said.

"I left it up there on the ridge, right behind Shelton's. I couldn't drive in any further with the snow."

I picked a blanket off the rocking chair and told Portis to turn around. I hadn't been to see him in months and took quick stock of the cabin. The sum total of his furnishings remained a cot, card table, and rocking chair, all of which were fanned out to face the woodstove. There were shelves built into the wall behind the stove and they were lined with whiskey fifths, canned food, and jars of jerked meat—which I guess made it the kitchen. Behind the furniture there was nothing but crates of clothes and supplies, then a window looking out on the pines.

"Carletta would call this an open floor plan," I said.

"There was no plan about it," Portis said. "Rick Potter built this cabin as a hunting shack. I won its rights in a hand of cards not long after me and your mother quit. But yes, to answer your question, I do like it open. It's better for energy flow."

I felt the warm air prickle my skin when I took off my T-shirt, then wrapped myself in the blanket and stood by the woodstove. I shivered and told myself to ignore the sour, sweaty funk of the blanket. I reminded myself just how cold I'd been only moments earlier, out there in the night.

Portis bounced Jenna lightly on an arm. He drank from the

whiskey and looked down at the baby from the corner of an eye. He puffed out his cheeks and made a farting sound. Jenna sputtered a bit, then cried a little softer.

"You don't happen to have a phone, do you?" I asked. "Cellular or otherwise?"

"No," he said. "I don't believe I do."

"Why does that not surprise me?"

"I don't know," he said. "But I'd love to sit down and discuss the matter further. I'd like to get to the bottom of your feelings on this issue, which are of great importance to me."

"She's calmed down," I said.

"She run out of things to say," he said.

"She likes you."

"You don't know nothing about it," he said.

I took Jenna and the backpack to the card table. Portis had a little stack of pornos there, and of course they were the worst kind of filth. Portis was a miser even when it came to the purchase of his smut. You could tell because the covers had all these tiny pictures of sorry models, like they didn't want you to look too close at any one.

I shoved that nastiness off the table and I could tell Portis was ashamed by how quick he gathered them up and stuck them on the shelf beside the canned food. I unfolded the blanket and set Jenna down on the table while Portis returned to his whiskey and lit a cigarette. He went to the door and peered out.

"I'll go get your fucking rice-burner Tonka truck," he said.

"It's a Nissan," I said.

"It is a product of the Orient," he said. "No matter what you call it."

"Uh-huh," I said.

I peeled off Jenna's clothes as careful as I could, but there was no stopping her scream. She yelled out and then for a few terrible moments made no sound at all. She just lay there with her mouth wide open, howling silent until her wind caught and she heaved and screamed again.

"My goodness," said Portis.

There were streaks of urine and shit down her legs and it turned my stomach to look at it. I might not have had it in me to shoot Shelton Potter, or anybody else, but I should have done something with the mother. She smoked herself under, then lay there like a carpet stain while her baby cried out in the cold. What I should have done was grabbed her sorry ass by the hair and dragged her to the police myself.

I took to Jenna with the wipes but she was already covered in rashy burns. Her bottom was blistered terrible and there were bumps at the diaper line that flared red and oozed. There were welts beneath a crust of dried shit on her back and when I looked at it in the light I felt my throat catch. I thought I was going to cry again.

"What is it?" said Portis.

"Will you come here and look?" I said. "Please."

Portis breathed in sharp when he saw and then I picked up Jenna's legs to show him the backside.

"Jesus God," he said.

"Do you think it's infected?"

"I don't like that ooze," he said. "I can tell you that much."

He had a pot of water warming on the woodstove and he dropped in a washcloth, wrung it out, and brought it back to me at the table. Jenna's cheeks were wet with tears and snot and I put my hand on her stomach to steady her.

She howled and kicked her legs while I wiped. I wanted to drop that cloth and hold her but I grabbed her ankles and kept on. She pounded the table with her fists and when she went purple in the face Portis had to step outside.

I put a fresh diaper on when it was over and then took some blue footie pajamas from the backpack. They were clean and dry and I buttoned her up quick. Portis came back in when the crying was over, read the directions for the formula, and fixed a bottle.

"I expect she's hungry," he said.

I sat at the table with Jenna in my lap and cooed at her while I shook the bottle. I was worried she wouldn't trust me after that diaper scene, but she snapped the nipple right up and drank.

"There you go," I whispered.

I watched her throat go up and down with the sucking and worried over how long she'd gone without.

"Go ahead then," said Portis. "Eat that up, little Jenna."

"She's hungry," I said. "That's for sure."

When she finally paused to breathe I wiped some runoff from her chin and for the first time she made a sound that wasn't crying—gurgling as she reached out to me with her hand and brushed it lightly against my chin.

"Did you say something?" I said. "Are you making conversation, Jenna?"

Jenna said *pthththth*. I said *pthththth* back, and then a smile broke across her lips and I saw the tiny, jagged edges of two teeth. Jenna said, *Ghuuuu.*

"Well *ghuuuu* yourself," said Portis, and leaned over the two of us.

"She's beautiful," I said.

"Generally," he said. "I find most babies tip toward the ugly side. Most of them look like Winston Churchill, if you want to know the truth. But this one here is cute as a button."

"As a button," I said.

"She damn sure ain't Shelton's," he said. "I can tell you that much right now."

Jenna wanted another bottle after she cashed the first one, but I imagined it could be dangerous to overfeed a baby. Especially one so hungry. For all I knew, Jenna was starved half to death. Her face and cheeks were fleshy and rounded, but otherwise she was paper thin—with the same bony, jutted elbows and knees as the mother.

I held her and burped her and before long she fell asleep and Portis was putting on his snowmobile suit and snowshoes. He poured off some whiskey into a flask, then drank from the flask and refilled it. He was going to get my truck.

He pumped the lever of his rifle and told me to play the radio loud if anybody came by.

"Leave the door locked and let the radio drown the baby out. Whoever it is will think I'm passed out drunk like always." He pointed to another rifle, hung from the far wall on nails. "They come in, it's within your rights to shoot them on sight."

"I'm not shooting anybody with this baby here in my arms," I said.

"Suit yourself," he said. "But I've always thought it better than being shot."

"Hurry," I said, and turned to look down at Jenna.

Chapter Four

Shelton Potter woke in the middle of the night, bothered by the smell of dead dog. Old Bo had passed a few days earlier and when Shelton sat up on the couch he quickly lit a cigarette and inhaled deeply, hoping the smoke would dilute the stink some.

Old Bo had died of natural causes, at least that was what Shelton assumed after he keeled over and died without providing much in the way of an explanation. Initially Shelton was too grief stricken to move the body, but now he wished he would have. Now the smell had found its way downstairs and he was frightened by the idea of what he might find in the room. Shelton did not like the thought of decaying dog flesh and wriggling maggots any more than he liked the idea of Old Bo being dead and gone forever.

The farmhouse was cold and drafty, but Shelton did not hurry to find a shirt. He preferred to flex his arm and give his triceps a little bounce. He'd been slacking on his workouts since prison, but generally Shelton was pleased with the progression of his triceps. His first love was the biceps, they would always hold the key to his heart, but that was no excuse to ignore the triceps entirely.

He dropped down to the floor, stretched his legs out, and planted his hands behind him on the edge of the couch. He knocked off twenty quick extensions, just to get the blood pumping.

Meanwhile, there was a Talking Heads song on the stereo. Shelton didn't care for the Talking Heads, they just happened to be on his uncle Rick's *Hits of the 80s* CD and that was what Kayla liked to listen to while they got wasted. The song was doubly irritating to Shelton now, but he didn't know where the remote was and the stereo was all the way across the room.

We've got a wild, wild life, sang the man.

Shelton finished his exercises and sat back down on the couch. He knocked some ash into his palm and readied himself to problem-solve, to figure out this whole Old Bo situation.

What he wanted to do was talk Kayla into dealing with the corpse. Kayla was a bleeding heart, and if he emphasized his grief, if he focused on the trauma he would suffer having to see Old Bo in his current state, then maybe he could elicit enough sympathy to get her to undertake the grisly task. In exchange he would offer to change the baby's diapers for an entire day, which would appeal to her shrewder, more rational side.

Speaking of the baby, Shelton remembered how they'd put her to sleep upstairs before they got high. Kayla had been worried about secondhand smoke. She asked if it was the same for meth as it was for cigarettes, could it harm you just by being near it? Shelton said it stood to reason that it could, and they did the responsible thing and took the baby to the second floor.

Shelton knew he should check on the baby right away, even if it meant walking by Old Bo. It was the right thing to do. Babies needed checking and the truth was Shelton sort of liked the little bugger. Jenna was cute as anything, and not too much trouble.

Of course, what Shelton really wanted was for Kayla to wake up and go get the baby herself. He could start a fire and Kayla could bring the baby downstairs for Shelton to hold. Then he and Jenna could sit nice and cozy on the couch while Kayla disposed of Old Bo's corpse. Afterward she could brew coffee and cook them up some pancakes. Then they could eat and share some of their fondest memories of Bo. It was a lot to ask, but it was Shelton's dream, and for a moment there on the couch he dared to dream it.

He nudged Kayla with a toe, but she was crashed. He got down on his hands and knees and checked her air and was comforted by the shallow, tender breaths she drew through her nose. Shelton kissed her on the forehead and whispered that he loved her. It was the truth.

"Now, let's see about this baby," he said, and stood up.

Shelton walked to the base of the stairs, where he paused to gather his courage. He picked a dirty T-shirt off the banister and slid it on. He pulled the collar up over his nose, and while the shirt stunk like sweat and hot piss it was no defense against the presence of rotting death. His eyes watered as he ascended the stairs and he gagged when he passed Old Bo and hurried to the end of the hall where they'd left Jenna.

Sometimes he called it the baby's room, just to see how it sounded, and he was grateful for the fresh air through the window when he finally pushed the door open.

"Good morning, sunshine," he said, but when he turned to the bassinet Jenna was gone.

It was a startling sight. Shelton had seen some things in his time, but he couldn't remember anything as awful as that little empty mattress and smooth bedsheet, right there where a baby should have been. But where could Jenna have gone? He knew they'd put her down in the bassinet because he specifically remembered opening the window. They'd done it so the smell from the dog didn't make her sick. He was sure of it, because he remembered that he and Kayla had debated the decision at length. She thought the cold would be bad for the baby, but Shelton insisted.

"This is science," he had said. "There's bacteria floating around in this air and the cold will kill it."

He had no idea if this was true or not, but it sort of seemed like it might be. Kayla eventually ceded to this logic and they put Jenna in the bassinet beside the open window. He remembered saying they'd be back in a minute and then heading downstairs to smoke some shit.

Shelton sat down on the floor and crossed his legs Indian style. It was the way he sat when he needed to think. He hunched forward and picked at the carpet. He was stupefied.

How long had he been passed out? And had the baby somehow gotten out of the bassinet and crawled away? As far as Shelton knew the baby couldn't crawl, but suppose it had learned while they were downstairs sleeping? Suppose the baby flung itself out of the bassinet and then all of a sudden figured out how to move? Suppose it went off on a little stroll? It didn't seem likely but Shelton couldn't be sure; he didn't know that much about babies.

Then he had a terrible thought. He had the worst possible kind of thought and hurried to the window and looked down. If the baby had flung itself out of the bassinet, then the odds were fifty-fifty that it had gone out the window side and plunged straight to the ground. And if it had plunged straight to the ground it would have long been buried by the falling snow. He looked out at the blizzard, felt the cold bite his knuckles on the windowsill.

"Jesus, no," he said.

He ran outside in his stocking feet, took a shovel from the porch, and started working through the drift beneath the window. He dug and with each plunge came closer to fathoming the horror he would suffer if he plucked the baby out of that drift with his shovel blade.

Shelton burrowed clear to the ground but there was no baby frozen in the snow. He dropped to his knees and looked up at the open window. He was flooded with relief and might have wept with joy, except the baby was still gone and he had no idea where. He left the shovel in the snow and went inside.

For a moment he considered calling Uncle Rick. Rick was on a Florida vacation and had asked not be bothered, but this might be a situation he'd want to weigh in on. Missing babies could be a problem for all involved, but on the other hand Rick had left Shelton in charge. His only instructions had been not to fuck anything up, and now that he had it didn't seem in his best interest to report it directly.

Shelton needed something to puff on, but there was no meth left in the house because he'd cooked the last and smoked it with Kayla. Kayla didn't weigh but ninety pounds, but the girl could smoke shit.

It always seemed Shelton ran out of meth at the worst possible time. He needed desperately to focus and began to panic at the prospect of attempting to do so while sober, but then remembered the tank of nitrous oxide he'd stashed in the closet, in case of emergency.

Well, if this wasn't an emergency then Shelton didn't know what was. And maybe a little nip of nitrous would be the perfect change of pace. There was more to life than methamphetamines and in truth it would probably do him some good to lay off the pipe for a bit, lest he begin to exhibit signs of addictive behavior.

He brought out the tank and stood it on the living room floor. He had a pack of party balloons to go with it and fished out a red one first. He turned the nozzle on the tank and savored the satisfying hiss as the gas discharged.

The beauty of nitrous was that it wouldn't show up on a standard piss test. At least Shelton didn't think it would. Obviously the methamphetamines would be there in full parade, along with the pot and the alcohol and the cocaine, but what good did it do anybody to dwell on such things? His PO could call him up at any moment and have him drive over to the courthouse to piss. That's just the way the legal system was, unorganized and flat impossible to predict. It wasn't something you could let get in the way of living your life.

He sucked down the first balloon and held the gas in for a bit before he breathed out. Then he filled another balloon. He swallowed the second and leaned back on the couch and felt his head go *wha-wha-wha*.

It was good to unwind every now and again, Shelton thought. A good snort of nitrous was like having somebody take a scrub brush to your brain, and he'd be damned if the world didn't sparkle for a moment there on the couch.

He did another balloon and then went into the kitchen and poured himself some vodka, but only to accent the gas. He wasn't going to get drunk, not at a time like this. All Shelton needed was a little warmer.

He picked up General Winthrop, the Maine coon cat, and promised himself that when the general died he would not leave his body in an upstairs bedroom to rot. He petted the cat and had his drink.

"You and me, Winthrop," he said. "We will walk through this world together."

The general let out a sigh and Shelton stroked his mane.

"Good boy," he said.

Shelton had begun to think somebody had strolled right into the farmhouse and stolen Jenna from her bassinet while he and Kayla lay there sleeping. Such a trespass was brazen and bold, it was half crazy, but it might be the only logical explanation for the baby's disappearance. It was either that or it had sprouted wings and flown away.

What Shelton needed to do, and he was ashamed he hadn't thought of it right off, was put up a reward for Jenna's safe return. Never mind that he didn't have the money. He could square that later with some help from Uncle Rick.

His uncle had half a dozen scumbags at his disposal. Career petty criminals and general dolts who'd been selling his pot and blow since high school. Of those slack-assed losers, Krebs was the most reliable and the first one Shelton phoned.

"We got a situation," he said.

"What's this we?" said Krebs. "You got a mouse in your pocket?"

"There's a baby gone missing," he said. "And it needs to be found. Pronto, Tonto."

"What baby?" said Krebs.

"It's a friend of the family."

"Whose is it?"

"Well, that don't matter now, does it?" said Shelton. "There's a baby gone missing and I need you to search out these hills and find it. It's what Rick wants, too."

"What happened to it?"

"It got took."

"By who?"

"We don't know."

"Where are we supposed to look?"

"Get on your sled," he said. "Drive up and down Grain Road and then head west. If you don't find her, circle back and do it again. That's what I'm going to do."

"I feel like there's not a lot of information to go on here," said Krebs.

"Maybe not," Shelton said. "But it's what we got."

"I'd feel better if we called Rick."

"I just talked to Uncle Rick. Uncle Rick don't want to be bothered any more on this. Uncle Rick said there's five thousand dollars for whoever finds this baby."

"He put out a reward?"

"Five large. Cash."

"Shit," said Krebs.

"That's what I'm saying," Shelton said.

"Do you know if it's a boy or a girl?"

"It's a girl."

"What's she look like?"

"She's got pretty black curls," Shelton said. "Greenish eyes. I'm not sure exactly. She mostly just looks like a baby."

"All right then," Krebs said. "I ain't been to bed yet anyway."

"Good," Shelton said. "Go ahead and get out there now. Don't wait for morning."

"I'm on it," Krebs said.

Shelton hung up and wondered if he'd gone a bit far with the reward money. Rick was rich, but that was because he didn't like parting with money. His uncle was going to be furious, but Shelton supposed he'd burn that bridge when he got there. The important thing now was finding Jenna.

Kayla stirred in the living room and it occurred to Shelton that the last thing he needed was for her to wake up and realize Jenna was gone. He could not handle her hysterics, could not risk her panicking and calling the cops.

He took a Valium from the vial she kept in her purse and crouched above her. He lifted her head gently from the floor and whispered that everything was okay as he tucked the pill inside her delicate, dry mouth. She mumbled something over the V and he hugged her close and told her to go back to sleep.

"Everything is fine," he said, and pried her mouth open to wash the pill down with a few gulps of vodka.

She coughed when she swallowed. She spat up some of the Gordon's but the pill stayed down. She leaned against him and he kissed her on the forehead and said he loved her. It was a tender exchange. A beautiful moment, he thought, if you looked at it in the right way.

He eased her back onto the floor and she drifted off without a peep. She never asked for a pillow, but Shelton took one from the couch and tucked it beneath her anyway. "Goodnight porridge," he said. "Goodnight spoon."

Shelton had another balloon and then one more. He didn't do it for the taste, but there was an edge of sweetness to the gas if you took a moment to savor it. Shelton smacked his lips and did another. And then some more. He didn't see the point in keeping count, but soon there was a pile of bright balloon husks at his feet. He did one more and then went to the closet for his snowmobile suit. It was black with a red racing stripe down the left side and it fit him nice and snug. He believed it accentuated his chest in a very subtle but powerful way and he had sprung for the matching helmet and boots. He did a balloon for each boot and then another one for the helmet. *Wha-wha-wha.*

He gave himself a look in the mirror when he was dressed and wished he wouldn't have knocked Kayla out so soon. He wished his girl could have seen him in his full winter sports regalia. Shelton was a sight, and he would not deny it in the name of false humility.

A snowmobile suit was like a tuxedo for trashy folk, and Kayla would have blushed red had she seen how handsome he could be when he took the time. It was his pectorals, yes, but what about that black visor? Shelton felt like a goddamn mystery in that visor, the sort of mystery a woman appreciated in a man.

But for all the suit's glories and the visor's intrigue, the helmet itself was the real gem. The belle of the ball, as they say. The helmet was aerodynamic, and its modern shaping concealed, or perhaps redistributed, the abnormal size of his head. Shelton had a big, swollen-looking head, which he was sensitive about because he thought it made him look retarded.

He had a learning disability, that much was true, but it was a long way from being retarded and Shelton hated that his head might suggest otherwise. As a child he was picked on endlessly for his head. In elementary school they called him Buckethead and Shel-tard. And while each name had its own cruel merits, his classmates consolidated their mockeries when Shelton grew a mustache in the sixth grade and everybody began to call him Gorilla Head Retard.

Shelton never fought back, despite a considerable size advantage. In fact he was usually the one who laughed the loudest at his own expense. Sometimes he jumped around and made monkey noises, scratched his armpits, and beat his chest. He couldn't help it, Shelton wanted everybody to like him so bad.

Had anybody ever spoken with Shelton about his childhood he might have told them he never quite escaped the echo of those schoolyard taunts. That he took them with him wherever he went, and heard them most clearly when he glanced in the mirror and saw that big head of his. But nobody ever spoke with Shelton about much of anything, let alone his childhood. Maybe that was why he'd nearly killed John Jameson, his drinking buddy, when he leaned toward Shelton at the bar and said, "Pass me that beer, Jughead."

Shelton's painful past was so long ago now, but in other ways it felt like it was still happening. Yet all those voices went silent when he slid his helmet on. Shelton looked good and thought maybe he should walk upstairs and a take a picture of himself in the full-length mirror, then text it to Kayla for when she woke.

The issue was he'd have to walk by Old Bo again. He'd have to smell him and remember that he was dead and deal with that whole gamut of troublesome emotions and he simply didn't have the strength to do it. Not now. Not when there was so much else to be done.

Shelton was ready to roll, but why in the world was that Talking Heads song still playing? And where was the damn remote? Shelton checked the coffee table and then patted the pockets of his snowmobile suit, which didn't make any logical sense. He'd just put the snowmobile suit on and the CD had been playing all along, so obviously the remote wouldn't be there. He checked the pockets again, though, just to be sure.

He went into the kitchen next and shooed General Winthrop off the table. The remote was not in the pile of dishes and dirty glasses and he looked at the cat and wondered if he might have run off with it.

"What about it?" he said. "Did you run off with my remote, General?"

The cat exhaled and settled into a curl on the floor. He licked at one of his front legs.

"No," Shelton said. "You might not be much, General Winthrop, but you are not a thief."

Shelton opened the refrigerator and closed it. He kicked the keg and it was empty. He paced the kitchen and then walked back into the living room. He squeezed some more gas out of the tank, took a balloon break.

He searched the coffee table again and then picked up the couch cushions and tossed them on the floor. He looked in the couch creases and then beneath the La-Z-Boy recliner. He looked on the mantel above the fireplace and then went back to the coffee table. He picked up an old, upended cereal bowl but there was nothing underneath it.

"Goddamn," he said.

He picked the couch cushions off the floor and set them back on the couch. He got on his hands and knees and crawled around the carpet. He ran his fingers through the shag and felt for the cool of the plastic.

He had another balloon and then went to the bathroom and looked in the toilet. He walked back into the kitchen and looked on top of the fridge and then inside the dishwasher. He kicked the keg a little harder this time and it was still empty. He opened and shut the pantry door and then walked into the living room.

The irony was, with all the energy he'd just spent he could have walked over and shut the damn power off by hand, could have done it a hundred times. Shelton realized this and felt like a fool, felt for a moment like he was still Gorilla Head Retard, jumping around the schoolyard and acting ape.

Then he looked at Kayla and thought it might disrupt her sleep to shut off the Talking Heads anyway, and what did he care since he was about to fire up the sled and go find Jenna? So it turned out the entire remote incident was a waste of time. Shelton told himself not to dwell on it and blew himself up another balloon.

Shelton had some joints rolled and tucked away in his top-secret drawer in the kitchen, which was also where he kept his Glock with the fancy laser sight. He grabbed the gun and a few hog legs for the road, then blew Kayla a kiss good-bye. He flipped down his visor and walked into the storm. If he didn't know better, he might have thought he was a hero.

Chapter Five

My feet got cold sitting there in the cabin, waiting. I thought it would be good to get out of my socks, to warm them for a bit by the stove, but I didn't want to move and risk waking the baby. She needed her rest and I needed the quiet. I did not like the idea of Jenna crying out while Portis was gone and Shelton Potter was out there lurking in the night. I felt lucky to have Jenna calm and was not willing to risk so much as a flinch if it might wake her.

I may not appear to be the feminine, caretaking type, but I have always been good with babies. I had the reputation around town as a tomboy, which is what they call you in Cutler when you don't wear makeup but are also not a lesbian.

My sister, Starr, had a new baby boy out in Portland and we were already thick as thieves. Tanner was only six months old and I hadn't met him in person, but I went to the library every

Saturday so we could Skype and I swear that baby wouldn't stop smiling once he set his eyes on me. Starr kept saying she would pay for my plane ticket if I came to visit, but I didn't have the heart to tell her I couldn't—that Mama had fallen off again and couldn't be left alone.

Starr and her husband, Bobby, had been out west about eight months and were just getting settled. Bobby's uncle was a big-deal contractor out there and had nothing but work for Bobby since they landed. They put a down payment on a house, with some help from Bobby's uncle, and the last thing I wanted was to worry Starr about what was going on back in Cutler.

Mama was sober when Starr left and I didn't see any reason to tell her otherwise. Starr wanted me to go with her, to move in with her and Bobby, but I told her we might as well pour Carletta a drink ourselves if we both took off and left her all at once. I told her we needed to give Mama a real chance to make it this time and she finally backed off when I swore up and down I'd call the second Mama slipped.

I never did call, though. Starr preferred not to speak to Mama directly, so whenever she asked I told her Carletta was doing fine and made up some bullshit about how she was still waiting tables and going to meetings.

I don't know if Starr believed me, but I don't think she wanted to outright accuse me of lying. Not when she was out in Portland with a new baby and couldn't do anything about it anyway.

The bigger deal was school. I hadn't been to class since October, when I went full time at the furniture store to keep Mama and me afloat. That was the one thing Starr would not abide. I was officially a high school dropout and if Starr found out she would go scorched earth and probably file for custody. Either that or drug my ass and crate-ship me to Portland herself.

I was thinking about Starr and how well she was was doing, about how much I missed her, when it hit me who the girl in the farmhouse was: Kayla Hawthorne. She'd been in Starr's grade all through school and a total train wreck from the jump. I didn't recognize her at first because she looked about a hundred years old, but the fact was she couldn't have been a day over twenty-two. Kayla Hawthorne had been to jail herself and already had a two-year-old in Porcupine County she'd lost to the state.

I looked at Jenna and realized how glad I was to have her with me. If I wasn't certain about that before, I was now. She was out of that farmhouse and safe in my arms and that was no small thing.

I listened to the creak of the floorboards beneath the rocker and lost myself in her slow, steady breathing. I watched the rise and fall of her chest and followed a few brambles of vein that traced down her neck. I listened to the firewood crackle and focused on the beautiful baby in my arms.

Eventually I fell out and must have slept hard because I'd forgotten where I was by the time Portis burst through the door all angry and soaked with whiskey. I sat up startled and found Jenna crying in my arms.

"You parked that truck on a goddamn slope," he said. "The snow just piled in there and set. It's up to the wheel wells, which isn't to mention that you're five feet off the trail to begin with."

"What?" I said.

"You're stuck," he said. "That truck ain't going nowhere."

"I thought I stopped in time," I said. "I didn't think I went in too far."

"You were wrong."

"Can we dig it out?"

"We ain't digging nothing," he said.

"I'm sorry," I said.

"Don't be sorry," he said. "We don't have time for it. But how many times have I told you not to park on a slant in the goddamn snow?"

"I don't know," I said. "I don't think you've ever told me that."

"That's bull," he said.

Portis stripped off his snowmobile suit and told me to pack some jerky in his rucksack. He told me to get two bottles of whiskey and pack those too.

"Where are we going?"

"Get the bottle of clean water," he said. "And take that for her formula."

"Portis," I said. "Tell me where we're going!"

"Hurry up and pack," he said.

Portis cut the hood off his snowmobile suit with a buck knife while I set Jenna down and packed the ruck. My hoodie and shirt were nearly dry on the woodstove and after I pulled them on Portis tossed me a sweatshirt.

"It's big," he said. "But it's clean."

It was baggy and gray. It said RESTORE THE ROAR above a faded Detroit Lions helmet. It seemed these were the woman clothes Portis had promised, and I pulled the sweatshirt on over my hoodie and winced a little at the smoke-soured cotton.

Portis had cut two holes in his hood and run them through with rope. He told me to come over with the baby, handed me the hood, and said to set Jenna down inside it. He looped the rope over my head, then arranged it on my shoulders. When I said the fit was right he tied it off. I looked down at Jenna, nestled and secure inside. She was no longer crying.

"That's your papoose," he said.

The crown of the hood was lined with fur and it made a nice edge and kept Jenna tight to my midsection. Her legs were dangling out a bit, but Portis fed them into a wool sock and said I could shield her inside the sweatshirt too.

Jenna gurgled.

"She should be warmer in this," he said. "Easier to carry."

"Portis," I said. "Please tell me where we're going."

"To my truck," he said. "And then to the hospital to get this baby some help."

"Why are we packing all this shit?"

"Because we've got to take the long way."

"Why do we have to do that?"

"I'll explain it while we walk," he said. "Being as it's the long way, we'll have plenty of time."

He handed me a flashlight and tucked some extra batteries into the pack.

"The storm's hit a lull," he said. "We can make decent time if we leave now."

"I'm sorry," I said. "For dragging you into this."

"Don't be sorry," he said. "You ain't dragging nothing. You done right when you took that baby, and you done right when you came to me. Generally, you always have done right. Whatever wrong you done been long canceled out."

"I don't know about that," I said.

"I do," he said. "Sure as anything. And either way it don't matter, it's my job to help you."

"Yeah?" I said. "Why's that?"

"Because," he said. "We were almost family once."

We walked into the dark and the night. I was none too happy to be back in the cold, but at least Portis was right about the storm. The snow had stopped and the wind was quiet along the river.

Portis had put the snowmobile suit back on and wore a knit hat where the hood had been. There was a trowel clipped to his waistband and a knife sheathed beside it. He carried a flashlight in one hand and a bottle of whiskey in the other. His rifle was strapped to the ruck with rope.

I had Jenna in the papoose and her backpack was slung over my shoulders. Portis led and I followed the trail his snowshoes carved along the bank. I kept my own flashlight pointed straight ahead and walked.

The long way to the truck meant we had to walk south to the footbridge and cross the river to get into the eastern half of the hills. Portis said you couldn't get back into that brush on anything but foot and that it was too dangerous to stay where we were, west of the river, or to try and get out on the main road. Portis suspected Shelton and his boys would be all over the trails shortly, assuming somebody cared enough to realize Jenna was gone.

Once we crossed the bridge we would hike northeast up the hill toward Trout Pond. Portis kept his fishing shanty there in the winter and said we would need some rest and warmth before we made the final push. His truck was parked at Scutter's Point, a clearing where the east and west sides came briefly together above the river. I'd been right about Portis being up there to check some traps, though he never admitted to the drunkenness I was sure had separated him from his old Ford Ranger to begin with.

Portis figured it was after two in the morning and that we'd be lucky to get the baby to the hospital by breakfast.

"It is my fervent hope that we will have this situation sorted before the lunch crowd arrives at the Elias Brothers," he said. "If I am in one of those luxurious vinyl booths and eating a farmer's omelette by ten A.M. then I will consider this little escapade of ours a success."

In the rush I'd forgotten to ask Portis for some wool socks. I knew one of us should probably go back for a pair, but I felt like an idiot for forgetting them and didn't want to slow us down.

There was no telling what Shelton might do if he caught up. People said he could be sweet, almost docile, but then his temper would flare and shit would get serious.

He'd done his year for nearly killing John Jameson at the Paradise Junction. They were drinking at the bar when Jameson said something to set Shelton off. Nobody knew what Jameson said, but twenty minutes later he was on a stretcher and Shelton was in the back of a squad car, cuffed.

Jameson spent two days in critical condition and in the deep quiet of my heart I had hoped for him to die. In fact, I'd never hoped for a thing so hard in my life. I was ashamed of myself but I couldn't help it. That hope was so deep and true that I couldn't beat it back—not even with my horror for having birthed it.

If Jameson died, and he was no model citizen himself, then Shelton went away, and maybe for life. They'd stop pumping so much crank out of the north hills and Carletta would have a fighting chance. There'd always be dope around, but I did not believe it was any coincidence that Mama's worst episodes always included Shelton somehow.

In the end Jameson pulled through. Children die of cancer every day and yet the black-hearted Jameson was permitted to carry on with his alcoholic drinking and pursuit of underage girls. I used to use this fact to fend off the Jesus freaks at school, who occasionally got so desperate for souls they decided to slum it and came trolling for mine.

Shelton did a year, and nearly fifteen months later—walking through the cold with Jenna bundled in my arms—I still wished John Jameson would have died. I wished it more than ever.

"I don't know where she could be," I said. "Mama."

"You'd do better not to think about it at all."

"Her car was right there at the farmhouse."

"Well," Portis said. "She was never one to stay put."

"I keep thinking she's froze to death, buried out here in a bank of snow."

"She's not frozen anywhere," he said. "Your mother's just off somewhere stoned. Like always."

I put my light on the river and I could see the water moving low and fast between the frozen patches. I could see the big trunks of the pines around us and the open spaces where the snowmobile trails cut through and it was clear why Portis wanted to get us across. It was going to be a long, hard trudge, but we needed to find some cover.

He was right about the river and he was probably right about Mama. She had a knack for surviving things she shouldn't, but more than that I knew I would have sensed it somehow if she were dead. I picked up calling her Carletta from Starr, but I still called her Mama, too. We were bonded like that, by blood and bone, by spirit, and I would have felt it the moment she fell away from me. It would have brought me straight to my knees.

Jenna was asleep and I watched the thin mist of her rising breath. I was glad she was resting but did not like the way her limbs hung loose in that carrier. I thought of how bad skinny she'd looked in her diaper.

"She's too scrawny," I said.

"Babies supposed to be fat," said Portis. "The fatter the better."

"She's malnourished."

"And that's a goddamn shame," Portis said. "I believe I could kill somebody, leave a baby alone like that."

"I don't even want to think about it," I said.

"The irony is," he said. "It happened to you just the same."

"Hardly."

"You don't think?"

"I never got left in a meth house, Portis. Not like that."

"Don't get too hung up on the details," he said.

"Details?" I said. "Or facts?"

"Child ain't the one supposed to be chasing after the mother," he said. "Supposed to be the other way around."

I felt myself tense, but fought the urge to fire back. Portis would never budge on Carletta and there was little profit in arguing the subject with him further. Besides, he'd never seen Mama sober and had no idea how good she could be when she was clean.

Just that summer she'd put together five weeks off of everything and I'd never seen her look so good. There was color in her cheeks and her hair thickened and bent into the curls I remembered brushing out as a girl. I wished Portis could have seen her, picking little blooms from the spit of weeds along our drive and tucking them behind her ears.

She made breakfast every morning and I'd sit at the table and drink my coffee while we idled away that lazy time before we both had to leave for work. Mama is from South Carolina and she was always going on about the ocean.

"I never thought I'd miss anything about the South," she said one day. "But I do miss the ocean."

"You like the ocean better than the lakes?"

"A lake isn't anything to the ocean," she said, and laid out some bacon strips on a paper towel. "A lake might look big from the shore, especially if you don't know any better, but you stand at the edge of the ocean and you'll see the difference. You'll feel it, too."

"Feel it how?"

"It's hard to describe. But it kind of makes you feel empty and all filled up at the same time. And after you leave the ocean, it sort of knocks around inside you. Like an echo. I haven't been back in fifteen years and I can still see it as clear as anything. I can see the piers stretching out and the storms coming in black above the water."

"I wouldn't like the salt."

"You'd take to the ocean the same natural way you take to everything, Percy. Which isn't to mention that the ocean is in your blood. You and Starr both."

"I'd like to go sometime," I said. "To South Carolina."

"We'll go," Carletta said. "My cousin Veronica still has a place down there. She's right on the beach, too."

Deep down I never believed we'd actually make it to South Carolina, but it was good enough to sit there for a few minutes and think that we might. To see Mama smile as she dumped some eggs into the bacon grease and worked them with the spatula.

I would have liked to stay right there in that memory for as long as I could, until we crossed the river at least, but my toes were hot inside my boots and it was becoming hard to ignore. There were flashes of pain and it was already clear not going back for the socks had been a terrible mistake. I started to wonder how long it took frostbite to set in, or if it already had. I'd been cold before, but this was different.

I shifted my weight to try and trigger some circulation, though I was careful not to draw Portis's attention. I felt foolish, but also feared he'd make me take the sock from Jenna and put it on myself if he found out I was hurting.

It was best to keep walking. Best to keep focused on getting to that bridge. Portis pushed ahead with his shoulders hunched forward and I blew some warm breath in Jenna's direction and hoped that it helped ease the cold some. I hoped it was better than doing nothing at all.

There was a clearing in the clouds and for a while we lucked into a bit of moonlight to walk in. I could see how wide the Three Fingers truly was, maybe twenty feet to the opposite side where the pines stood like a wall and held back the deep forest. The river sounded like a snare drum where it rushed and when the water broke the bank it would spray high and dimple the fresh powder.

Portis had picked up his pace and I sped up to keep close behind him. I was about to ask him about the bridge, about how much farther it was, when a light swept through the trees behind us and I heard the high whine of a snowmobile.

Portis dropped to his knees and I followed suit. Then the light drew back and the forest went dark. The drone receded and for a moment it was still and quiet in the woods. Portis looked over at me.

"We'll run if it comes back," he said. "And if it comes to it and I have to stop to deal with Shelton, you keep running."

"What do you mean, deal?"

"It don't matter," he said.

"I'm staying with you," I said. "I'm not running if you aren't."

"Goddamnit," he said. "You'll do what you're told."

The light returned in full and the glare was wide and bright and filled the forest with shadow. I didn't know who it could be but Shelton, and he was louder and closer now. Portis told me to kill my flashlight and I stood when he did and ran hard behind him down the river.

There was a thump in my feet with every stride, like a hammer dropping, but I did not slow my pace and ran through the pain as best as I could. The light swept back and forth behind us but I could not tell if we'd been spotted.

Portis cut hard to the left when we came to the bridge and I could see it stood about six feet above the river and that it stretched straight and long through the dark.

I followed him out onto the warped wood and took an unfortunate glance to the right, where the handrail was collapsed and the snow tapered into a smooth sheet of ice. If I slipped it would be a straight shot into icy water and I did not want to think about what would happen if I were dunked and caught up in the current.

Jenna was crying hard in the papoose and I clutched her close to my chest and ran with my eyes cast down. I watched every stride land and did not look up to get my bearings or to glance behind my shoulder to see if Shelton had closed in. I can promise you no straighter path has ever been run, and while you could credit me with some triumph of balance, in truth I was just too damn afraid of falling.

I was so focused on what was beneath me I was late to notice when Portis called out, when one of the planks snapped beneath him and he fell through to his knee. I didn't see he was down until I was right on top of him and I would have gone ass-over-teakettle had he not reached out to grab my waist and pulled me in.

I slid some in the snow but when I steadied he let me go and told me to run. I stood for a moment and watched him struggling to free his leg.

"Go!" he shouted. "Get the hell across this bridge."

I saw Shelton's lights cutting through the woods and when I reached for Portis he slapped away my hand and told me to get.

I did not want to leave him there, but I did. I ran to the other side and then collapsed into the snow on my knees. I was wheezing but I tried to calm Jenna between breaths.

"Portis!" I said.

"Keep going, Percy," he said.

"Where?" I said. "It's all trees."

"Just walk off the bridge a little ways. Wait for me up there."

"I could come back out and try to pull you."

"Shit," he said. "This whole fucking bridge feels like it's about to go."

"What happened?" I said.

"What do you think happened? I stepped through."

"Are you in the water?"

"No," he said. "My foot is dangling."

The light had grown softer and more distant across the river. I was quiet for a few moments and listened until I could no longer hear the sled at all.

"I think Shelton's gone."

"He might be," Portis said. "At least for the moment."

"What are you going to do?"

"Stay here," Portis said. "And become one of those pieces of human installation art. What do you think I'm going to do?"

"I'm serious," I said.

"Good," he said. "I'm glad you're serious, because I'm just fucking around. I'm just out here for the fun of it."

Jenna had slowed her crying some and I looked down and told her that everything was going to be fine.

"It's okay, Sweetgirl," I said.

Portis grunted something awful then, grunted loud and long and then screamed out as the bridge wood crackled. I sat holding Jenna and watched the woods over the river.

"Portis," I said. "Are you out?"

He didn't respond, but I could hear his boots clomping, and when he finally joined me on the other side he was drinking deeply from his whiskey bottle.

"Are you okay?" I said.

"Compared to what?" he said.

"I don't know," I said. "Your usual self."

"Compared to my usual self I am just fine. Though less drunk than I may prefer."

Portis had torn through the left leg of his snowmobile pants. I put my flashlight on him and there was a brightly bloody gash that ran up and down his thigh.

"Jesus Christ," I said. "That might need stitches."

"It's fine," he said.

"Do you need to take a break?"

"You are welcome to," he said. "But I will keep walking."

"Are you sure?"

"I'd like to put a little distance between us and what's on the other side of the bridge," Portis said. "I believe I'll feel better when we are relaxing in the warmth of my shanty."

"How much further is it?"

"A few klicks."

"What's a klick?"

"It's hard to explain."

"We need to take a break soon," I said. "Don't walk us all the way to the shanty if it's much further."

"Well," he said. "I guess I've been told."

"I'm serious, Portis."

"That was established on the bridge," he said.

Portis turned and kept walking and I was heartened by his rudeness, which was in keeping with his character and calmed me some about his leg. I was also glad to see that he was not favoring it too noticeably as I followed him onto what appeared to be a foot trail.

The walking was much tougher in the thick woods and all of it was at an incline. There was barely room to spit, yet alone travel by sled, and that was fine with me. We followed the short beams of our flashlights and I felt a little bit safer with each step we took away from the Three Fingers.

I walked and was glad to be with Portis and to have slipped right into the old, easy way we had always known together. I hadn't seen him since the summer but when it came to Portis and me it was always like no time had passed at all. As a little girl I used to hope the good parts of Portis would beat out the bad, and I believed all these years later that they had.

I was seven the year we lived together and could still picture that Portis clearly, the one with a trimmed beard and black locks of hair spilling from the sides of his baseball cap.

He moved into the little apartment we had on Petoskey Street and after school me and Starr would come home to find him sprawled on the couch with his Viceroys and the television. He loved *Welcome Back, Kotter,* and when he wasn't bringing us up to speed on Barbarino's antics or reenacting one of Horshack's punch lines, he used the commercial breaks to regale us with stories of the summer he spent in Mexico. *Mex-ee-co,* he called it.

There had been lots of boyfriends, especially then, before Mama really turned. I could barely keep one man straight from the next, except for Portis, who was funny and harmless and forever combing his fingers through his bushy mustache.

Carletta didn't tell me or Starr shit about our own father. Only that we shared the same one and that he had left us high and dry when I was still in the womb. Carletta guessed he had moved back to Colorado, where she said he likely continued to not give a damn about anything but himself.

Starr said you had to take everything Carletta said with several grains of salt. Starr said we were born five years apart and how could we have the same father if Carletta never stayed with anybody, other than Portis, for longer than a few months? And did Mama think Starr wouldn't remember a daddy that had hung around for five years before suddenly bolting for Colorado?

I'm sure Starr was right, and what did it matter anyway? If anybody was my father it was Portis, and he only lasted a year before the night Mama kicked him out. I can't remember what they fought over and I'm sure it doesn't matter, but I remember looking out at the rain after he left—beading on the windows and falling fast through the yellow light of the streetlamps.

I marked the moment as the beginning of Mama's unraveling, though Starr said its significance existed mostly in my mind. Starr said I only remembered that night because I was so young and because we had liked Portis so much. Starr said Mama had been unraveling long before he split.

"If she was ever even raveled in the first place," she said.

I liked being with Portis, but it always came with a tug of hurt when I thought of everything we might have had, everything we might have been if only him and Mama had lived different lives and found a way to stay together through it.

The east side of the river felt much safer, but we were moving slow. The snow had deepened between the trees and I had to use the pines for balance and move from trunk to trunk. I was starting to lose feeling in my toes and between the numbness there were stabs of heat and outright burning. The pain came in waves, and when a bad one hit I had to stop myself from crying out. I found that if I put my weight on my heels it helped slightly, but it made walking that much more difficult.

There was no longer any light from the moon. The sky itself might have remained lit, but there was no way to tell through the high canopy. I felt about ready to collapse and was glad to see Portis finally drop his ruck and cop a lean against a tree. I stopped beside him and we both stood there breathing heavy.

"Goddamn," he said. "That's a tough sled."

"It's like walking through molasses," I said.

"Yeah," he said. "Except it's cold as shit."

Portis uncapped his whiskey and had a gulp. He had another and then offered me the bottle.

"You want a nip?" he said. "For the warmth?"

"No," I said. "I'm fine."

"Good girl," he said, and had another.

Jenna cried some and I wondered if I should take her out. I knew she wanted to be held, that she was likely hungry, but thought it might be best to keep her sealed inside the carrier. That whatever warmth had gathered needed to be held.

Her eyes were hard-creased at the corners when she cried. The tips of her black hair were frosted with snow and the tiny mists her breath made in the cold tore me up with their smallness. I'd known that baby no more than a few hours and she'd already broken my heart a half-dozen times.

"She seems to be holding up," Portis said.

"It's amazing," I said.

"We'll feed her at the shanty," he said.

"How much further?"

"Not much," he said. "We'll get there before the storm hits again."

"What?"

"This storm's about to take things up a notch," he said.

"It's not even snowing."

"Well," Portis said. "It's about to."

"I think the storm has passed, Portis," I said. "I haven't seen a flake of snow since the cabin."

"This storm's a long way from over," he said.

"How can you tell?"

"It don't matter," he said, and held out his gloved hands. "C'mon. Let me carry the baby for a bit."

"I don't know if I can carry your pack," I said. "It probably weighs more than she does."

"I didn't say you had to carry any pack."

"I'm fine with her, Portis. Really."

"I ain't going to drop her," he said. "Hurry up and do it while she's still fussy. That way we only have to settle her once."

"What about your leg?"

"What about it?" he said, and left his hands held out between us.

I was too tired to fight him any further. Besides, my shoulders were on fire and I was desperate for a break from that carrier. I lifted it off and handed Jenna over.

Portis's hair fell forward off his brow and as he gathered Jenna close he pushed the strands back to keep from disturbing her. He put the harness over his right shoulder and swung the papoose in and carried it like a football. The rope was too small to loop across the other side, but Portis barely seemed to register the weight as he folded his left arm beneath the right and walked.

Jenna fussed harder at first, but her cries soon steadied and then receded altogether. She fell asleep in Portis's arms and I felt the muscles in my shoulder and back loosen and go to jelly.

"Portis," I said. "Can I ask you something?"

"You can," he said. "But only because I don't think I can stop you."

"Did you ever think about asking Mama to marry?" I said. "When you two were together?"

"Well," he said. "This took a turn."

"It's something I've always wondered."

"I thought about it," he said. "Sure."

"How much?"

"Who knows?" he said. "A lot, I guess."

"Then why didn't you?"

"No reason, really."

"There had to be some reason," I said.

"There wasn't."

"Did you love her?"

"I did."

"She was pretty, wasn't she?"

"She was as beautiful a woman as I'd ever seen. And I have not seen one like her since."

Portis, though prone to hyperbole and outright fictions, was telling the straight truth about Mama's looks. I have a picture of Carletta when she was my age, outside her papa's house in a summer dress. She is in a field and there are wildflowers scattered in the tall grass—the chicory and primrose blooming while she stands there and looks like she just strolled off some Hollywood set.

Mama's been up north for years, but she's from the South and still sounds like it. She used to say I was her rebel daughter because I talk like her, while Starr talks northern. I never considered my speech to sound like anything, but I could hear the difference between Mama and Starr.

Either way, she split her good looks evenly between us. Starr got the breasts and the blond hair, while I got the blue eyes and height. The flip side of that coin is my bird chest and black hair, while Starr is cursed with stubby legs. If Mama was a ten and we both came out sixes then it's pretty clear our daddy, or daddies, whoever they were, contributed little of value in the looks department. Which was exactly what they contributed in the rest of the departments.

"So why didn't you ask her?" I said. "To marry you?"

"I told you the truth," he said. "When I said there wasn't no reason."

"That doesn't make any sense."

"I might have thought there was a reason at the time. But if I can't remember it now it wasn't much of a reason, was it?"

Portis had stopped walking.

"Here it is," he said.

I couldn't see the shanty in the dark but I could tell we'd come to the edge of Trout Pond. I could feel the open air and the absence of the pines.

"The shanty's out there?" I asked.

"It's out there," he said.

"Is it safe?"

"You've fished with me in that shanty before. I don't recall anybody falling in."

"I'm talking about Shelton," I said. "He won't come back here looking?"

"Shelton's lazy ass?" Portis said. "No. I don't think he will hike out to find us on this pond. Of that I'm nearly certain."

"Certain would be better," I said.

"Best not to start thinking about what's better," he said. "That's been my finding."

Chapter Six

Shelton rode his Polaris 500 from the Three Fingers River to the easternmost edge of the north hills and searched every nook-and-cranny trail on the way. He was twenty-five years old and he'd been riding sleds near his entire life, but he still felt that same old boyish excitement with the sled fired up and roaring beneath him.

One thing was for sure: they had needed the snow. Shelton had been disappointed in the snowmobiling so far this season, but then the storm came and winter had been reborn in the deluge. Yes, there was a baby to find, but there was also fresh powder and the hills' vast tangle of trails to explore. Shelton wasn't saying it made up for Jenna being gone, just that things weren't all bad if you knew how to look at them.

His mind was crystalline in the cold air and he could not remember the last time he'd seen such good sledding, certainly before Ionia and the entire winter he missed in the pen. He moved freely through the poplar and paper birch, rode the wide trails with everything electric and purely white in the high beams.

Shelton rode and eventually let his mind slip from Jenna. He forgot about Kayla unconscious at the house and Old Bo being dead and gone. Shelton rode until he forgot even himself.

He shot beautiful white sprays of snow and slalomed through the trees. He stood up on the straightaways to stretch his back and then sat back down and gunned it even harder. He sang bits of the rock-and-roll anthems of his youth, the classics that Uncle Rick had raised him on before all that business with the Talking Heads. Zeppelin. AC/DC. Humble Pie. Shelton did not do this consciously, or even realize it was happening. He would simply hit a little jump or take a tight corner and belt it out: "Thirty days in the hole!"

Shelton rode and rode and rode. He rode until the night drew back above the north hills and bled out slow, until he could see a rise in the distance where the pale stars were like a scatter of river stones and morning dawned above the pines with a bluish tinge.

Shelton believed it was as pretty a thing as he had seen, that edge of cold sun, that strange arc of light, and he hammered the sled and thought he might ride straight to the top of the hills and launch himself. He wanted to see if he could touch the sun, if only for a moment, and he believed he might have if the sled had not seized and then sputtered to a halt in the middle of the trail.

"Shit the bed," he said.

He started the sled back up and the engine turned, but she never got back to speed and when she petered out the second time it was for good.

"Goddamn," he said.

He wiped the frost away from the gas gauge and there was the needle, on that bright red, block-letter E. He stepped off the sled and looked around. He'd been on a southeast jaunt, toward the highway, and he was a long way from the farmhouse.

He couldn't believe he hadn't even bothered to check the gas. He was a damn fool and he had failed Kayla and little Jenna, which wasn't to mention Old Bo up there in that dark, cold room. Shelton might have cried, he felt so low all of a sudden.

He wished he had figured a way to bring that nitrous tank with him. He wished he could have a party balloon out there in the woods by himself, or at least a little pint bottle to tug at in all his sorrow.

He pulled off his helmet and threw it down into the snow. He wiped some snot from his nose and felt the cold bite the tips of his ears. He yelled out for help, but there was no answer. He called out for Kayla, too, and when she didn't respond he yelled that he loved her and that he was sorry.

He understood he was coming down now. Coming down hard. Crash, crash, crashing. He felt the blackness descend, felt the emptied-out lowness and dread. His heart was suddenly torn to shreds and his nerves were as hot as crackle wires. The problem with drugs was they didn't last forever. They gave you the wings to fly and then up and took the sky away. Mayday, mayday, Shelton thought. Black Hawk down.

He ripped off his gloves, threw them at his helmet, and unzipped the front of his suit. He took a few deep breaths and then slid his hand to his beltline and pulled the Glock. The laser came on by itself when the weapon was gripped to fire, which always tickled Shelton. It was a pretty red line, and bright against the snow, but in this instance purely ornamental; he wouldn't need it once he put that barrel to his temple.

One thing about that big head of his: easy target. One pull and it was done. He wouldn't have to worry about getting back to the farmhouse, or how he was going to have to explain to Kayla that Jenna got took while they were asleep.

Shelton adjusted his grip on the handle, felt the soft rubber, and wondered, would it hurt? He thought it might, if only for some fraction of a fraction of a second. He kind of hoped it would, though he couldn't say exactly why.

He wondered if there was a heaven and if he somehow got in, would Old Bo come running up to greet him with a ball to play some fetch?

Shelton doubted there was a heaven, though, and even if there was, he wasn't likely to get in. And even if he did, say on a clerical error, why would Old Bo come running up and want to play?

He wouldn't. Not after Shelton left him there to rot in that godforsaken coffin of a bedroom. So that would be it. Shelton would be dead and suffering an eternity of loneliness worse than he'd known here on earth.

All of a sudden it didn't seem like much of a choice. Not with Kayla back at the house and all the promise their love still might hold, if he could only get her baby back.

Then Shelton remembered he had a few joints tucked away in his pants pocket and that about sealed it. It turned out he would not be shooting himself in the head after all. What Shelton would do is fire up a marijuana cigarette and walk down to the highway to see if he couldn't hitch a ride. He was too far from the farmhouse to trudge back through the woods, and most of it uphill to boot.

Calling Krebs and the boys for help was simply out of the question. The boys didn't respect Shelton as it was, and he could only imagine what they'd say if they found out about the sled and how he'd run her out of gas. Shelton was supposed to be in charge, but in his brief tenure he had already managed to lose a baby and strand himself in the woods.

There shouldn't have been anything to be in charge of in the first place. Everybody bought from Rick and then sold at their own discretion, there was no real organization to it, but his uncle loved him and wanted to give him a vote of confidence and so he told the boys he'd be speaking through his nephew while he was gone. That if Shelton said he needed something they should treat it like it came from Rick directly.

Shelton was just out of prison and he'd done right by his uncle when he snitched out a competitor to plea down. Now that he was out and trying to make his way in the world Rick was repaying his loyalty, even if he didn't profit from, or care for, his nephew's product of choice.

Shelton smoked his joint and sat for a while in the snow. He was in the middle of a break in the trees and he tipped his head back to take in a bit of the sky above. The clouds were coming in low and fast and Shelton swore he bore witness to the very moment the storm returned, as if the norther had waited to make sure he was watching before it erased the dawn and its valiant crease of light.

Then the snow came. And the wind. Somehow, it felt personal. Shelton put his helmet back on and made for the highway. He must have come farther south on the trail than he realized because it wasn't long before he reached the road. The wind pushed harder in the open and the snow was whipped off the ground until he couldn't tell it from what was falling. There was one advantage to the bad conditions, though: Shelton figured people would be more likely to give him a ride if they couldn't see through the blizzard and tell that it was him.

Shelton had never seen such a storm. He'd watched Lester Hoffstead track her all week and while the weatherman had seemed downright histrionic, if anything Shelton believed he'd undersold the storm's wrath and devastating power.

She came down from Canada across Lake Superior and hit the Upper Peninsula first. Munising and the sandstone cliffs. Then she pushed inland and bleached the hayfields and the pines and balsam firs, the great emerald forests, the evergreen spine of Michigan's vast and big-hearted peninsula. She was slowed some by the trees but pushed through to Lake Michigan anyway, to Mishigami, the great water, where she rallied on the cold, black depths and finally struck Cutler in a full-blown rage.

Yes, Lester Hoffstead had done them all a disservice. Lester Hoffstead should have done everything in his power to whip his viewers into a panicked frenzy. He should have stood on his head and flapped his arms like a chicken, then read a chapter from Revelation while the camera panned across his Doppler radar.

Speaking of the Bible, Shelton had come to feel a bit like Jonah, trapped in the belly of the whale. It was as if the storm had swallowed him whole, especially now that he was beyond the trees on the highway, where everything was flat and folded into the violent, swirling gray.

He hated the storm, but he respected it, too, as he turned his back to the wind and stuck out his thumb. And miracle of miracles, the first truck he saw pulled over to pick him up.

It was Zeke Turner in his F-150. Shelton could tell because who else but Zeke had a pickup painted so brightly purple that it shone through the storm like a giant Easter egg. Shelton ran to the passenger-side door and Zeke hit the auto locks and waved him in.

"Get in, man," he said. "It's cold as a witch's titty out there."

Shelton shuddered as he climbed in the cab and Zeke tilted the heating vents in his direction.

"Thanks," Shelton said, and pulled off his helmet.

Zeke Turner had always been a stand-up guy. He would not deny Shelton a ride even if he'd been in prison for ten years. Shelton considered him a friend, or as close as he came to one.

"I thought that was you," Zeke said. "I couldn't tell exactly through the snow, but then I said, who else could that big motherfucker be out here by the hills but Shelton Potter?"

"I thought the same thing," Shelton said. "I knew it was you right off, because who else has a pickup that looks like a big ole gay Easter egg."

"Shit," Zeke said. "You find an Easter egg that isn't gay, you let me know. I'd say gay and Easter egg go hand in hand."

"Which begs the question," Shelton said.

"The purple is to draw your attention to the signage on my side panels. ZEKE TURNER ENTERTAINMENT."

"Okay," Shelton said. "Well, that actually does make some sense."

Shelton remembered then that Zeke was a singer. Or at least he was trying to be. Mostly he worked at the plastics plant, but he had dreams of his own, which would also explain why he was wearing a black cowboy shirt with white piping and sequin swirls stitched into the collar. He had on matching black pants and snakeskin boots. He wore a straight-banged black wig that sat on his head like an inverted bowl.

"You ain't wearing a coat?" Shelton said.

"Can't crease the shirt," Zeke said.

"You got a show then?"

"Rock and roll," Zeke said.

"Where at?"

"All the way to the Sault."

"Even in this storm?"

"Slot machines are inside," Zeke said. "I'm playing the brunch buffet."

"You look like Elvis," Shelton said. "But I know you ain't."

"Roy Orbison," he said.

"That's right," Shelton said. "I'm sorry."

Zeke waved him off.

"I get it all the time," he said.

They drove into the flurries and the freshly dropped sky. There wasn't another car on the road.

"It wasn't snowing," Shelton said. "And then, boom!"

"I saw two flakes come down all innocent, and then the fucker just opened right up," said Zeke. "It's like the planet Hoth out here."

"Well, I appreciate you stopping," Shelton said. "And I got a little doober for your trouble, if you're interested."

"I would say I'm keenly interested," said Zeke.

Shelton lit the joint and passed it to Zeke first. Zeke had a toke and passed it back. They smoked the joint quietly, deliberately. Shelton looked at Zeke and tried to decide if he was wearing makeup. He thought he might be. He thought it was strange for a man to put on makeup, but supposed things were different in the entertainment industry. He pinched the joint off at the roach and dropped it in the console.

"For after the show," he said.

"You're all right, Potter," said Zeke. "And I've never said otherwise."

"This is pretty good pot," Shelton said. "It's decent anyways."

"I'm going to crack the window a smidge," said Zeke. "But only because I can't tell the smoke from the snow."

"If you don't mind," Shelton said. "I could use a ride home."

"Sure," Zeke said. "What happened that you're out walking in this mess anyway?"

"My sled run out of gas."

"That sucks," said Zeke.

Shelton shrugged.

"You know you could come up to the casino if you wanted," Zeke said. "Sometimes there's some women to be had. Divorcées mostly. If not, I know some of the waitresses. We could get a room and see if we can't make a day of it. People up there like to party. I met a couple once and the husband wanted me to fuck his wife. It was like a Robert Redford situation."

"Robert Redford?"

"From that movie. Where he wants to fuck Woody Harrelson's wife. Except this was opposite because this guy wanted me to fuck his own wife. He was going to watch and requested I keep my wig on and there wasn't no money involved. It was not a paying proposition."

"Did you do it?"

"Hell no."

"Too weird?"

"Too weird," Zeke said. "But also 'cause the wife was ugly."

"If she was hot, would you have?"

"I can't say I wouldn't have."

"Yeah," Shelton said. "That's probably the deciding factor."

"So what do you say? You want to come up and see if we can't wreck some shit?"

"It sounds good," Shelton said. "But I've got some things to do around the house."

"Yeah," said Zeke. "I know how that is."

"How's your old lady?"

"June?" Zeke said. "She's mean as ever. I think she's fucking somebody else. She's always online hammering away at the keyboard, then when I come in the room she closes out the screen. Thinks I don't notice."

"That's too bad."

"She comes and goes. There's whole days I don't see her."

"Does she go to your shows?"

"Hell no," Zeke said. "She thinks the whole thing is childish.

She can't believe a grown man wants to spend all his time pretending to be someone else. That's her word for it, 'pretending.' "

"She don't support you?"

"No," Zeke said. "She doesn't. Not anymore."

"I had a girl like that once," Shelton said.

"She's got me trapped," Zeke said. He gave his collar a gentle tug, adjusted the line of the flare in the rearview.

"Sometimes I feel like life don't have no point to it," Shelton said. "If you want to know the truth."

"I feel like I've been living underwater," Zeke said. "Like I can't hardly breathe."

"You're drowning," said Shelton.

"The saddest part is, I've started to question myself. That's the real tragedy."

"Sometimes when I'm happy," said Shelton. "It don't seem real. Sometimes the sadness is the only thing that feels true."

"What's true," Zeke said. "Is that June left me a while ago. She left me without ever leaving the house. And I have no idea what I'm going to do about any of it."

"Life ain't what they made it out to be in school," said Shelton.

"That's a fact," Zeke said.

"My girl will probably leave me soon," said Shelton. "If I don't find her baby."

"Do what, now?"

"My girl, Kayla. Her baby went missing here last night. I was out on the sled looking for her when I run out of gas."

"What do you mean, a baby?"

"A baby," said Shelton. "In diapers."

"Went missing?"

"I woke up and she was gone. Like she just up and flew away."

"You're kidding me."

"Gone," Shelton said. "She got took is what happened. That's the only thing I can figure."

"Shit," said Zeke. "That's fucked up. Wait. Are you being serious right now?"

"As serious as I can be."

"I'm starting to feel a little stoned, so I'm trying to make sure I'm understanding all this correctly. You say your girl has a baby in diapers and that it has gone missing here this morning and that you think it has been abducted? Like somebody come and took it?"

"It happened last night sometime," Shelton said. "But, yeah. That's exactly what I'm saying."

"And you're not fucking with me?"

"I would not," Shelton said. "Not about this."

"Hell's bells," Zeke said. "I just seen a special on this. On television. There was a special investigative report. It had to do with the human slave trade."

"Slave trade?"

"Sex slaves, man. Like these sick fucks steal babies and sell them down in Mexico. They raise them up to be prostitutes."

"In Mexico?"

"It's an international trade," said Zeke. "But it's big down there in Mexico. Mexico and Russia. Those are the main two on account of their economy and general lawlessness."

"Motherfucker," Shelton said.

"And we've got all these fucking wetbacks now, man. All those spics over on Detroit Street. They practically own East Cutler."

"Grease Cutler," said Shelton.

"El Cutlero," said Zeke.

"But those Mexicans are cool," said Shelton.

"I'm sure some of them are," Zeke said. "I'm just telling you what I seen on the television. What was on the investigative report. You know any of those boys over there?"

"I know Little Hector Valquez. He does some work for me. He's a good kid, man. He moves a good amount of dope for me."

"Well, that would be where I'd start," said Zeke. "I'd go and ask that boy a couple of questions if I were you."

"Shit," Shelton said. "He does know about Jenna. I had Kayla and her with me last time I was over there to make a drop."

"Who's Jenna?"

"The baby."

"Damn," Zeke said, and shook his head. "You can't trust nobody."

"Motherfuckers," Shelton said.

"I'd go with you," Zeke said. "But I can't miss this gig, man."

"Don't even bother with the entry road," Shelton said. "Just drive me as far up Grain as you can, then I'll walk in the long way and cross the lake."

"I'll take you up, man. It's no bother."

"You can't get in the back," Shelton said. "Not in all this snow. Quicker if I walk in."

"How you going to get back out then?"

"I'm going to drive right out across the lake."

"Will it hold?"

"It'll hold," Shelton said. "I was out there doing donuts a week ago."

"You sure you don't want me to drive up and see if we can't get in? I still have faith in the 150, Shelton. I'd hate to think you didn't."

"It's not like that," Shelton said.

"They didn't take the bailout," Zeke said. "People forget that, but they didn't."

"I can't say that I would choose a Ford," Shelton said. "That's not something I can truthfully put my name to, but I can say that I think they have made some strides in recent years. Obviously I would never paint a vehicle purple, but I have no business reasons to do so."

"As long as it doesn't have to do with the truck."

"This is strictly about time," Shelton said. "Rest assured."

"Shelton," he said. "Can I ask you something, man? It might seem a little funny but I feel I need to ask."

"Shoot."

"Have you been wearing that helmet the whole time?"

"I wasn't at first, but then I put it on here a minute ago."

"Thank God, man. I thought I was losing my damn mind."

"You're straight, Zeeker," Shelton said. "And right here is good."

Zeke stopped the truck, but didn't even bother pulling off the road.

"Are you sure?"

"I promise you," Shelton said.

"I can't see a goddamn thing."

"Neither can I," Shelton said. "But I know where I'm going."

"I'll come by in a few days," Zeke said. "Make sure all this turned out."

"It'll turn out," Shelton said. "I'll turn it out myself."

Chapter Seven

Portis handed me Jenna when we got to the shanty, then lit a kerosene lamp and hurried to load his stove from a small woodpile in the corner. I hadn't been inside the shanty since middle school, but as the light flickered on I realized it was exactly as I remembered it.

The walls and floor were unfinished plywood and they were stamped with the Indian head from the Big North lumber company. Portis had a Packer stove that was short and flat and vented through a little hole in the roof, and there was a cot and a lawn chair along opposite walls. There was a pile of clothes in the corner and a milk crate full of gloves and hats. Between the clothes and the stove was a fishing hole where Portis worked at the ice with a hand auger. The whole place smelled funky, like wild animal, but like Portis himself was undercut mercifully with alcohol—an astringent, if nothing else.

We had tried to shield Jenna as best we could but I could see now that her cheeks were burned red from the cold. She wasn't complaining, though. Somehow she was as calm as she could be, just lying there in her papoose like we were at a Sunday school picnic.

Portis looked over at me as he cranked the auger.

"Change that baby's diaper," he said. "And then we'll deal with you."

"Deal with me?"

"Don't be a jackass," he said. "We don't have time for it."

"I don't know what you're talking about," I said. "But okay."

"You've been walking on your heels because you can't feel your toes," he said. "You've been hobbling around like a goddamn penguin all night, thinking I can't notice. Acting like I'm blind or a fool, either one."

"They're just cold," I said.

"You're frostbit, Percy."

"I don't have any frostbite," I said.

"Then I am the greatest swordsman in all of France."

"What?"

"Nothing," he said. "Just change the damn diaper." Portis was through with the auger and kneeled to scoop the pile of ice shavings into a green, ten-gallon bucket. He took the bucket outside to empty it, then flipped it over to use for a seat. I feared he had cleared the hole to shit in it, but he cracked the seal on his second bottle of whiskey instead. He smoked a cigarette and seemed contented for the moment.

I hated to upset Jenna with her so still in my arms, but I knew she needed changing. Portis was right about the diaper and it seemed to me that he might be right about the frostbite too— though I did not allow myself to linger on the thought of what his field remedies might include. There were two wool blankets folded up behind him but I did not want to ask him to grab me one. I didn't want him to think I couldn't walk over there and get it myself.

I braced myself before I stepped but couldn't help my wobble. I gritted my teeth and stepped again and when I grunted Portis stood up from the bucket.

"Hurts when it warms, don't it?"

He handed me the blanket and sat back down.

"Piss off," I said.

"Don't be mad at me," he said. "Be mad at your toes."

Portis tipped up his bottle and drank from the whiskey. He sat on his bucket and stared at his little piece of ice-cleared lake.

I spread the blanket on the floor and whispered to Jenna. I told her everything was going to be just fine.

"Just change the damn thing," he said. "Get it over with."

"Okay," I said, and took a breath.

I unzipped the onesie, then offered my finger to Jenna. She gripped it and then looked up at me and said, *dun-dun.*

"Hi, Sweetgirl," I said. "I see you."

Her eyes were as blue and as clear as pool water and I swear her vulnerability blew a tunnel clear through my chest. I wiped some spittle from the bottom of her lip and she said, *Thththth.*

"I'm so sorry," I said, and unhinged the diaper.

She flinched when the cold air hit, then looked at me in wide-eyed betrayal. Her chin wavered, then caved. She kicked her legs and flushed purple and I had never heard such terrible screaming, such honest-to-goodness hurt. It was like the screams came from some hidden depth, like they surprised her, too, and her whole body vibrated on their sharp-cut treble.

The welts were red and hard in the cold. They were still oozing at the diaper line and I hurried to put the dry one on.

"Baby girl," I said.

Jenna heaved with breath, then cried out louder.

I fit the new diaper, zipped the onesie back up, then held her to my chest. And she sobbed for some time like that, with her shoulders going up and down as she wet my shoulders with spit and snot.

"Sweetgirl," I said, and patted her back.

Portis had stood up from his bucket to look down into his hole. His jaw was clenched and he looked stricken.

"How in the world can that child's mother not have any diaper cream?" he said.

"That's pretty low on the list of her failures," I said.

"How bad is it?"

"Bad," I said. "Worse than it was. I think she needs antibiotics."

"Too bad she don't need decongestant," Portis said. "Plenty of that around these hills."

"I don't know what could happen," I said. "I don't know how long she's been infected. We're running low on that formula, too. I feel like we need to get her to the hospital, Portis."

Portis ground out his cigarette on the plywood floor, then went to fix Jenna a bottle with the jug water.

"Her diaper was wet," I said. "Really wet. We should have changed her earlier."

"Wet is good," Portis said. "Wet means she ain't dehydrated."

He handed me the bottle and Jenna took it through her crying and eventually it calmed her. I sat on the cot while she fed and Portis drank his whiskey.

"I can't take it," he said, and wiped some runoff from his chin. "When she cries like that."

"I know," I said.

"I've never been angrier in my life," he said. "Than when I hear that cry."

I leaned back against the wall and pulled the blanket up around Jenna. The fire was roaring in the stove but outside it seemed the storm had returned. The wind had reached a full-on howl and I couldn't see a thing through the window—a square foot of glass already buried in the snow.

Jenna was on her way to sleep in my arms. Portis put the papoose on the woodstove to warm it and I wondered if there was anything holding the shanty down. I wondered if we could get blown clear across the lake in the wind, but decided not to ask.

"Don't get too comfortable," Portis said. "You're next."

"I don't think you have to worry about me getting too comfortable," I said.

"Good," he said. " 'Cause we're going to get right to it."

"Get to what?"

"This little footbath you're about to get."

There was a water-boiling pot hung from a nail on the wall and Portis took it outside, the wind howling and snapping the door shut behind him as he went to gather snow. I felt sick inside, like this was about to be some Civil War medical tent type of business, the sort of shit they don't put on the postcards about Cutler County in the winter.

Cutler lived on the summer tourist dollar, but there were fudgies in the winter too—downstaters named for their willingness to drop coin on a particular top-shelf confection. Cutler will always have its beaches and ski hills, but is just north of prime cherry country and so its primary exports remain fudge and the Petoskey stone, which is an interesting and uncommon stone, the state stone in fact—but is mostly just a stone. Still, people went in for it. They bought their fudge and rock ornaments and for a few weeks in December it was all winter wonderland time in northern Michigan.

Downtown was empty now, but it was hopping when they had the lights strung and carolers wandering up and down Mitchell Street. There were wreaths on the streetlamps, stands for hot cocoa with marshmallow floaters, and the football team in Penn Park selling trees. You walk around town in December and it starts to feel like you're in a Dolly Parton Christmas movie—those are Carletta's favorites—but when the fudgies go home for the season the city cuts the power to the twinkly lights. They board up the big houses along the bay and there's nothing left in Cutler but the locals, everybody bracing for the real winter to set in and bare its teeth.

Fudgies get all misty over a white Christmas and they're always snapping selfies in the snow—but the real winter is months long and it will gnaw your goddamn toes off if you let it.

Portis came back inside and dumped a little water from the jug into the snowy pot, then set it on the stove beside the papoose.

"She's got to come to a boil," he said, then snagged a fishing pole. He baited the hook with a cigarette butt he'd blunted earlier, dropped the line in the water, and plopped back down on his ten-gallon bucket. He had a drink of whiskey and set the bobber. I could not believe my eyes.

"Jesus Christ," I said. "Are you fishing right now?"

"All along I have planned to fish when we arrived."

"We don't have time for you to fish."

"I believe we do," he said. "I believe that water is yet to boil."

"You have got to be kidding me, Portis! We need to get this baby some help and I swear I can't believe you'd even consider fishing at a time like this."

"Why'd you think I cleared the ice?"

"I don't want to say. I don't want to give you any more bad ideas."

He exhaled dramatically.

"Don't do that," I said.

"Don't do what?"

"Breathe in that manner. Attack me without having the balls to do it directly."

"Are you now telling me how to breathe?"

"No," I said. "I am telling you how not to breathe."

"Jesus, God almighty!" he said. "Can you let up for one damn moment? Can you let me sit here in peace and fish? Can you please allow me that simple pleasure for the next five minutes?"

"You haven't even dealt with your leg," I said.

"What would you like me to do to my leg?"

"You should pour some whiskey in it to sterilize the wound, then wrap it to keep off the cold."

"That is an offense to the whiskey," he said.

I dropped my head in my hands and breathed out.

"Now you are the one exhaling," he said.

"I thought you had a plan," I said.

"This is the plan!" he said. "We are resting and safe from the storm. We are waiting for that water to boil. And while those things happen I would like to wet a line and I refuse to believe that is a problem in any way whatsoever. Despite your harassment."

"Harassment?"

"This is a cross-examination," he said.

"That's a little dramatic."

"No, it is not. It is not dramatic in the least. I think you would make a fine prosecutor of the law, Percy James. I can see you now. One of those fire-breathers in a man suit, stomping around the courtroom and scaring everybody shitless with your short haircut and meanness."

"Maybe you should try some bait."

"You don't know nothing about it."

"What don't I know? That you can't catch any lakers with a Pall Mall filter?"

There was steam billowing from the pot on the stove and I could feel the heat push toward me from the fire. Portis was right: my toes hurt worse the warmer it got, and I braced myself by gripping fistfuls of blanket when he wasn't looking.

He leaned his rod against the wall and watched his bobber

while the whiskey bottle hung loose from his hands. I could see that he was thinking on something heavy. I could tell by the way his brow arched up and made his face narrow and mean.

"I am a fine fisherman," he said.

"I've never seen you catch a fish in my life," I said. "Nor have I ever seen a picture of you with a fish in hand."

"Watch your mouth, missy," he said. "I am well known across three counties for my expertise and skill as a fisherman and have likely slain more steelhead than any man you have ever met personally in the flesh. I caught two, I repeat two, twelve-foot sturgeon in the summer of nineteen and eighty-eight."

"You didn't catch any sturgeon."

"I surely did."

"That seems like something I would have seen a picture of. Maybe in the newspaper, even. But I have seen no such pictures."

"This was before the advent of digital technology," he said. "People could not take pictures with their goddamn phones. So while it is true that there are no pictures to commemorate those victories I implore you to go down to John Parlee's bait shop and ask him who caught the two biggest sturgeon he's ever seen. He will say the name Portis Dale."

"John Parlee sold the bait shop and moved to Florida," I said. "It's a realty office now."

"That is a vile lie."

"It is not a lie," I said. "John Parlee met a woman on the Internet and moved to be with her in Lakeland, Florida. They were matched on eHarmony and he has been baptized as a Christian on her request and conditions."

"You may cause my death," he said. "Right here in this shanty I may finally give out and die of pure sadness."

"I'm sorry," I said. "But it's true."

"How do you know?"

"Because I fish with actual bait, which means I frequented Parlee's. We spoke often. He knew of my association with you and yet never mentioned a single sturgeon, let alone two in the same summer."

"Go ask Big John the Indian then. Find him over there on the Bear River Bridge this fall, when the salmon run. He was there the day I caught the first one. He will also speak to you about the second one, which he undoubtedly knew of through hearsay."

I propped myself up on an elbow and tried to ignore the sound of the water boiling, tried to pretend my eyes were not watering from the terrible burning inside my boots. I had touched a sensitive nerve with Portis and was beginning to feel badly. I began to apologize in my roundabout way, but Portis cut me off before I got to the part where I said I was sorry.

"Shut up and take off your shoes," he said. "That water is long boiled and I'm through with your distractions."

He put his gloves back on and went to the stove, then picked up the pot and set it on the floor. I sat there and watched it steam while he pushed open the shanty door and grabbed a few handfuls of snow. He dropped the snow in the pot and then looked at me.

"Get on the floor," he said. "And don't debate me on this."

"What are you going to do?"

"You're a smart girl," he said. "I think you can deduce the basics of the process."

"Why'd you boil it, then put the snow in?"

"I boiled it to sterilize it. The snow's to bring the temperature down a bit. You don't treat frostbite with boiling water."

Portis took the papoose off the woodstove and walked over to set it on the cot.

"This is nice and toasty now," he said.

He took Jenna from my arms, put her down in the carrier, and then pushed the cot up against the wall. He nudged my shoulder and told me it was time.

I eased myself onto the floor and sat with my legs stretched out in front of me. I turned away while Portis unlaced my boots, then jerked when he went to remove the first one. It hurt like hell and I tried to wriggle free, but he grabbed my knee and held it to the ground while he pulled the boot clear off.

I clenched my teeth and grunted. There was sweat beading on my face already and I felt a flutter of nausea rise. He tugged the second boot off and when he peeled the socks away I pounded the floor with my fists.

"I know," he said.

"Do you!"

"I can imagine. Let's just rest now for a second."

I breathed out, looked down, and saw my toes were so purple-tinted and swollen, they looked like some damn eggplants. I let a whimper go and closed my eyes.

"It's like a picture in a medical book," I said.

"Bad as it may seem," he said. "This is still a before version of that picture. There's something worse comes after this."

"Is it frostbite?"

"Yeah," he said. "This qualifies."

"Am I going to lose my toes?"

"No," he said. "Not if we get them in this water."

"How hot is that water?" I said.

"What's it matter if your toes already burn?"

"Just tell me."

"I don't know," he said. "Hot. But we'll let it sit for another minute."

"How bad is it going to hurt?"

"I expect it'll hurt pretty bad," he said.

Portis took a drink of the whiskey and then offered me the bottle. I refused, but not because I'm a martyr, or some anti-liquor crusader. I would have drunk the hell out of some wine coolers or peppermint schnapps, anything to dull the pain or distract me, but whiskey makes me puking sick and I wasn't ready to introduce that specter to the situation.

Portis reached out to help me stand, then slid the pot in front of me.

"When you step in," he said. "Don't thrash around and go ass over elbows. If this water dumps, we got to start all over and do it a second time."

"I'm going to try not to scream," I said.

"It don't matter if you do or you don't. Just don't wiggle."

"I don't want to wake Jenna. She'll be frightened."

"Okay," Portis said. "But you scream out if you need to. Jenna will be fine."

"Goddamn it," I said.

"I know."

"I don't want to do this."

"You'll do it just like Jenna did her diaper. You'll get through what you need to get through."

"I can't believe I didn't have on better socks."

"I can't believe you didn't say nothing."

"I didn't want to slow us down."

"That was a stupid thing to think."

"I don't want you taking the sock from Jenna."

"I got some spare wool socks right over there in a crate," Portis said. "We'll get you and Jenna both squared away."

"All right," I said.

"Before we get started," he said. "I thought I'd share something with you."

"Share something?"

"Yeah," he said. "You see, this whole situation reminds me of something that happened once down in old *Mex-ee-co*."

I looked down at Portis but he had already lunged at my right ankle and lifted it without warning. I almost fell backward but he took me by the front of my shirt as he plunged my foot into the pot. The air froze in my lungs and I lurched forward as he pushed my left foot in beside the right. I grabbed his shoulder and screamed.

Portis held both my ankles sturdy. He grunted and cursed the burning himself, but did not so much as flinch. I tried to move but I might as well have been roped to concrete blocks. I couldn't quite believe how badly it hurt.

Portis was saying something about Mexico. I could barely hear him, but I focused on the sound of his voice and tried to listen through the pain and my own cries.

"I was a young man then," he said. "Full of wanderlust. I had drifted deep into the heart of the country, the real Mexico, which ain't what it looks like on the postcards."

Portis was breathing hard through his nose. I knew that water was burning him something terrible. I was sure some had leaked inside his gloves and pooled there, but he kept his grip steady and went right on talking.

"It ain't no Jimmy Buffett song down there," he said. "I can tell you that much right now. There's no fishbowl margaritas or Señor Frog T-shirts. This was the real Mexico, a place of dust and brown water. There was heat and violence and snakes and coyotes. It is a hard place full of hard people and I was on the trail of Montezuma's gold."

There were tears streaming down my face and I was shaking from my middle, from some deep and usually still place that had been dug up in the pain. Maybe it was the same place Jenna had cried from just a little while before, and the thought of her strength helped me as I closed my eyes and told myself to focus on Portis's fool story.

"I was traveling with another gringo," he said. "Name of Henderson. He was an expat, a paramilitary type who'd done dirty work for Reagan in the Sandinistas. Somewhere along the line he read some Carlos Castaneda and discovered peyote. He met a village girl, became a pacifist, and eventually renounced the United States as imperialist aggressors.

"Henderson had been searching treasure for near a decade, but mostly what he did was smoke peyote. I smoked some with him, somehow got separated, and woke up several days later on top of a dirt mountain. I was naked and deep fried to a crisp.

"Who knows how I got up there on that crested plane? Who knows why I was unclothed? I was looking for gold, and Mexico is a land of many mysteries. But there I was. Passed out for hours, maybe days.

"Now, that was a burn, Percy James. Put your little toes here to shame. I'm here to tell you, I had welts and yellow pus all over me. I looked like the damn elephant man. I twitched and I shook. I had an erection that could not be reasoned with."

I sputtered out something that was both a laugh and a cry and he kept on.

"I walked for half a day, barefoot on burning sand. I was cherry red and sailing at full mast. Lord God, was I a sight. Finally, I arrived at a village and was taken in by a kind family, who I believe to this day I owe my life.

"They provided me a bedroll and a spot in their thatched hut. And when I had a peek at myself in a shard of reflective glass I busted out crying. I about died, is what happened.

"I was later told by a doctor that I had suffered a stroke. This doctor's counsel was given at a roadhouse, and while he later confessed to being unlicensed and I never received a proper examination, his reasoning has always struck me as sound.

"Anyway, the village family prayed over my body and treated me with a strange green liquid, served in a wooden bowl. I drank the mixture and vomited profusely, but when I woke my erection had finally been resolved and I no longer twitched. The village elders assembled, and while they were glad I was on the mend they asked that I leave in the morning. Apparently there was some talk that I was with the devil. *Con el Diablo.* This was six months before I returned home and met your mother."

I opened my eyes and looked down at Portis, who looked up at me and smiled.

"Margaritaville," he said.

My knees had gone to sand and I slumped forward and hugged him. I sobbed as the burn turned back to a throb and echoed out.

Afterward, Portis wrapped my feet in a blanket and lifted me onto the cot.

"It still hurt," I said. "But I appreciated the story."

"That's all right," he said. "I didn't even have to make much of that one up."

"I could have done without the erection detail."

"That was no detail," he said. "Trust me. That right there was the feature presentation."

"I take it you didn't find gold?"

"The gold remains buried."

"What happened to Henderson?"

"He disappeared into a puff of peyote smoke. I never saw him again, and there are days I wonder if he ever existed at all."

I arched my toes gently and made myself a promise that I would save up some cash for a proper pair of boots and get myself some good wool socks. I promised I would never play so fast and loose with their fate.

Meanwhile, Jenna was still asleep in the papoose and I liked lying there beside her, in the warm and the quiet.

"My sister always says babies are tougher than they look," I said. "That they're tougher than we are."

"This one is," said Portis. "I can't say about other babies, but we got us a trooper here. I like this Jenna. I'll admit to it."

"She's so quiet, though. Maybe too quiet. Like she's sick or something. Like she's too tired to cry."

"She was hollering pretty good there a bit ago," he said. "When you changed out her diaper."

"Yeah," I said. "I guess she was."

"She's eating and she don't seem to have a fever," Portis said. "She's alert. When you get worried about a baby is when their eyes go glassy."

"I thought you didn't know much about babies."

"I don't," he said. "I know about glassy eyes."

I put my hand to her forehead and she did not feel hot or clammy. There was still color in her cheeks and she slept with her lips parted and her head turned. Her chest rose with breath and her tiny hands were relaxed into half fists at her side. She was the prettiest thing I'd ever seen.

"She's so beautiful," I said.

"She's a bright light shining," Portis said.

"She must be so tired."

"That makes three of us."

"I don't feel too badly," I said.

"You need to rest before we go for the truck."

"I can walk."

"You think you can," he said. "But right now you need to rest. Even if it's only for a bit, to let this storm pass. Then we'll walk out."

"I don't like just sitting here," I said. "It makes me nervous."

"There's no place safer in these hills," he said. "There's nobody even knows about this shanty. I don't even bother with the padlock."

I heard Portis shift on his bucket. I heard the flick of his lighter and his deep draw on a cigarette.

"How is your sister?" he said.

"She's great," I said.

"And the baby boy?"

"Perfect."

"I'd like to meet the little sailor one day. Bring him up here to the hills and take him fishing."

"He'd love it," I said.

"We need to do it while he's young," he said. "Before he becomes corrupted by the Pacific Northwest and their generally sissified ways."

"You don't know a thing about Portland," I said.

"And for good reason," Portis said.

"I feel like I've been hit by a truck," I said.

"I might take a rest myself," he said.

"Okay," I said. "But we can't let ourselves sleep too long."

"I don't ever do," he said. "My demons won't allow it."

"Portis," I said. "Will you do me one favor and let me see your leg? You might be frostbit yourself."

"My leg is fine," he said.

"Then bring it here."

He labored to get off the bucket and walked over. He extended his leg and I could see that the cut was deep but that the skin was not otherwise discolored and that Portis was probably right— just a bad gash.

"Will you wrap it at least?"

"Consider it done," he said, and plopped down on the floor with a blanket.

Portis blew the flame from the lamp and we all lay there in the dark. The shanty was rippling with dry stove heat and I watched the orange ember of Portis's cigarette burn. I watched the smoke trail off into the black.

I held Jenna's little hand and listened as Portis began to sing quietly to himself. His voice was gravelly and low and he sang something about shame and the moon. Something about blaming it on midnight. I closed my eyes and fell asleep to the sound of his voice and the firewood crackling.

Chapter Eight

Shelton returned home and watched the storm through the bay window while he worked the nitrous tank. He was going to town to see about Little Hector, but not until the morning barrage let up a little.

In the meantime, he was glad for Kayla's ability to sleep through a crash. You heard stories on the news about people sleeping for three straight days when they came off, but you didn't think it was possible until you saw it firsthand. Well, he had seen it now. Kayla was lying there like a dead person, hour after hour. It was amazing, Shelton thought, what the human body was capable of.

He remembered Krebs then. He'd dispatched him last night, but it occurred to him now he hadn't seen anybody else out on the trails. He called Krebs and could tell by the sound of his voice that he'd just woken up.

"Shit," Shelton said. "You didn't even go out, did you?"

"Man, I'm sorry," said Krebs. "I sat down here on the couch and must have fell out."

"Goddamnit," Shelton said. "I was out there looking all night."

"Did you find her?"

"No, I didn't find her. Why would I be calling you if I found her?"

"I don't know," Krebs said. "Maybe to tell me to stop looking."

"You weren't looking in the first place!"

"It's an academic point," Krebs said. "I admit."

"You got to get out there," Shelton said.

"I'll do it," Krebs said. "Just as soon as this storm settles down. I'm going to call Arrow and see if he wants in. Maybe Clemens too."

"I can see Clemens," Shelton said. "But what do you want with that crazy fucker Arrow?"

"I owe him for this other thing," Krebs said. "I figure this is a good way to square us. He'll appreciate me cutting him in."

"Well, that five thousand is a lump sum. It don't go to every one of you, individually."

"I know," Krebs said.

"You'll have to figure that out amongst yourselves. In terms of the split."

"We'll handle the technicalities," Krebs said. "You heading back out?"

"I'm going to wait this storm out myself," Shelton said. "Then maybe head into town in the truck."

"You got a lead?"

"Too early to tell," Shelton said, and cut his phone off.

Shelton thought it wise to keep Krebs ill informed. He might be in cahoots with the Mexicans for all Shelton knew, and even if he wasn't it was a better deployment of his resources to keep him in the hills. Krebs wouldn't do him a damn bit of good in town, and if they did find Jenna with Hector, as Shelton suspected they would, why would he want Krebs riding his coattails for the reward money that didn't actually exist?

He looked over at Kayla on the floor and she was so lovely and still. He got down on his knees beside her and ran his fingers through her hair and then rested his head next to hers on the carpet.

The Talking Heads were still on the stereo, which came as a surprise to Shelton. How had he not noticed it before? He'd been sitting in the house for twenty minutes, probably heard the song five times, and was just now realizing it was there? Shelton supposed it was the nitrous and the general stresses of the situation. His mind was elsewhere, literally.

And what was there to do about it now, with him so comfortable on the floor and the stereo so far away? Shelton closed his eyes and vaguely understood that he was about to fall asleep.

Chapter Nine

I don't know how long we slept in that shanty, but the storm had eased and I felt rested when I woke. I drank some water and Portis forced me to eat a plug of jerky, which I hoped was venison but tasted like a smaller game I did not need specifics on. We packed up and were gone.

There was some gray light above the hills as we left the ice— Portis in the lead and me trailing behind with Jenna babbling in her papoose. The snow was piled high on the pine boughs and the woods were still beneath the fresh powder as we walked back into the trees. I was glad to see Portis had wrapped an old T-shirt around his wound, though I doubted he'd bothered to clean it with the whiskey. Baby steps, I thought.

"It's pretty," I said. "But I swear I am never coming back up on this hill."

"This hill is cursed," said Portis. "There isn't a doubt."

"You're the one that lives here."

"I don't so much live as I do exist."

"That's deep."

"I wish it were," he said.

The Packer stove had given me my feet back. They were snug inside the wool socks and I stepped on them freely and without pain. I had been warmed all the way through by our time in the shanty but now that the cold had returned it was damn blunt about it. Like it hurt even worse because I was still so near to the alternative.

"How long was I out?" I said. "In the shanty?"

"I don't know."

"Can't you tell it by the way the snow falls or something? By the way the light slants? Mountain man that you are."

"Of course I could," he said. "But what does it matter? Time don't move in a straight line up in these hills. It sort of wiggles around and folds back on itself. There's no way to put a number to it."

"Whatever that means," I said.

"It means what it means," he said. "It ain't a riddle."

"I'm just curious what time it is?" I said.

"Roughly, nine in the A.M.," he said.

"I guess we're not making breakfast," I said.

"I did not factor in frostbite and another dumping of snow into my calculations."

I looked at Jenna sleeping and was heartened by her calm and the soft touch of color in her cheeks. For the first time since I found her I had a solid feeling inside, like we were actually going to get her to the hospital.

"How far to the truck?" I said.

"A mile or so."

"That's not bad."

"It won't feel like any mile you've ever walked. I can promise you that."

"It's tough walking," I said. "But it can't be but so bad."

"We're going uphill the whole way," he said.

"It doesn't seem like it."

"It's a gradual incline."

"That's good," I said. "Gradual is good."

"You say potato," said Portis.

I could see him swaying a little as he stepped, but I figured it was from the labor as much as the drunkenness. Portis had been walking drunk near his entire life. Portis always said the key to walking drunk was to try and walk crooked.

Up ahead I watched as a swarm of chickadees broke from a jack pine, scattering tiny mists of snow as they searched out neighboring trees. And that's the thing about Cutler—it's a hard place, but sometimes it's so damn pretty you don't know what to do with it all. Portis drank from his whiskey bottle and I trailed behind him.

I tried to lose myself in the rhythm of the march. I tried to remain focused on how good my feet felt and to be grateful for their return. I was feeling better about our situation, that much was true, but it was hard to hold on to that feeling when the cold started to creep back in.

I had never considered myself the adventuresome type, and this entire ordeal had only confirmed that fact. You will not find me in any of those mud races, or leaping from a perfectly good airplane to prove some vague point about the human spirit. I do not relish risk or seek thrills and cannot understand people who pay their good money to endanger and punish themselves. You got to have it made to even think like that, to walk around feeling like your life needs a few more challenges thrown in.

I wish they had a website for such people. Rich folks with a bunch of crackpot energy. People like me could post help-wanted ads and then the adrenaline junkies could do something of actual value with their foolishness. I mean, why run through some mud you put there on purpose when you could come to Cutler and rescue a baby from the drug-ravaged farmhouse of a fucking lunatic?

I was getting a little loopy out there in the woods, thinking about how we could turn the whole thing into a race. I pictured a bunch of those X Games, Lance Armstrong types milling around Shelton's porch with their heart-rate monitors and protein shakes. I was cracking myself up good—imagining the Sandra Bullock moms in numbered running tights—when I heard the sleds in the distance and stopped cold.

There was more than one this time, but they sounded far away and muted—like flies buzzing in a windowpane.

"Do you hear them?" I said.

"Yeah," he said. "I hear them."

"It sounds like two."

"Yeah," he said. "It does."

"Where are they?"

"I don't know," he said. "Somewhere across the river."

I hurried to catch up to Portis and yanked on his coat to get him to stop walking. I figured that if we could hear them, they might be able to hear us, say if they stopped their sleds all of a sudden. It didn't seem to make much sense to stand there hollering at each other up and down the hill.

"Do you think it's him?" I said.

"Probably," Portis said. "Probably Shelton and one of those retrobates that run with his uncle."

"Shouldn't we be hiding or something?"

"I already told you they're across the river."

"They sound pretty close to me."

"Well," he said. "They ain't."

"How can you be so sure?"

"Because there's no way to get a sled back here, which I already explained."

"Still," I said. "I feel like we should do something."

"There isn't nothing to do."

"Shouldn't we at least move off the trail?"

"You're welcome to leave what's left of this trail," he said. "But I think I'll keep going this way."

"I don't like it," I said. "It makes me nervous."

"Well," he said. "You go right on being nervous and not liking it. Let me know if it changes anything."

"What's wrong with you?" I said.

"Nothing's wrong with me."

"Then why are you being so testy?"

"Am I being testy? I'm sorry, Percy. As your cruise director I deeply regret any momentary discomfort my tone may have caused you."

"Why do you continue to be an asshole?" I said. "When it's so clearly unnecessary?"

"Why do you continue to question my authority?" he said. "Why do you continue to question my knowledge of these hills and their inner workings?"

"I think its fine to discuss things," I said. "You don't have to take it all so personal."

"There is nothing personal about it. I know what I am doing and so I am walking on this trail and you are making me stop to explain things, as if to a child. I find it irritating that I have to parse everything so that it may be understood."

"You used to be nicer, you know?"

"And you used to be quieter," he said. "You used to be a sweet little girl, with ribbons in her hair. You used to be uncorrupted by feministic aggressions."

"I don't even know what that means. You sound like a babbling fool, Portis."

"And I believe I've sustained quite enough of your character assassination in these past hours," he said. "I've grown tired of your subterfuge."

"Whatever."

"Whatever is right," he said.

He stomped off down the trail and I gave him some distance. I did not let him leave my sight, but he was far enough away that

I was spared his huffing and puffing—his dramatic exhales of whiskey-drenched breath.

We made the rest of our walk in nearly that exact same terse silence. I could feel the burn in my butt and thighs and was under some considerable strain but only shook my head and kept walking when Portis asked if I wanted him to take the baby.

Jenna was as calm as she could be. She mostly lay there and blew spit bubbles, almost as if she knew I was upset and kept quiet out of consideration. She was the type of baby that I thought might be capable of exactly that sort of wisdom and kindness.

The buzzing came in and out but eventually I told myself Portis was right and almost talked myself into ignoring it altogether. I thought about Carletta and the summer and why I was out there in the hills to begin with. I remembered how she told me it never snowed in South Carolina.

"I remember it once or twice," she had said. "But it never stuck. Everybody ran outside to catch the flakes on their tongues and acted crazy."

We were at the kitchen table again, eating scrambled eggs and buttered toast. Carletta had a cigarette burning between her fingers while she pushed her coffee mug in little circles.

"There were hurricanes, though," she said. "Hugo was a bad one, but I was gone by the time it hit. I left not a month before."

"I saw pictures of those houses they build up on stilts," I said. "The ones on the beach."

"That's to keep out the flooding," she said.

"It seems crazy. To live in a house like that. Like any wind could just come up and blow you away. Especially with the storms."

"I expect they're as safe as anything else," she said. "You don't hardly even notice them when you live there. They've just always been there, so you don't even think about it."

"Is your cousin Veronica's house up on stilts?"

"I don't know," she said, and knocked some ash onto her empty plate. "I never asked her."

"I hope not," I said. "I don't know if I could sleep in a house on stilts."

"We'll camp out on the beach if you want," she said. "We'll sleep right there in the dunes one night."

"That sounds nice."

"It's as beautiful as anything," she said. "You should see the stars out above a Carolina beach."

Like I said, I never really believed we would make it to South Carolina, but six months later I was traipsing through the north hills because I still thought we might make it back to that kitchen.

Up ahead, Portis had finally stopped walking and pointed to a clearing just down the trail.

"Scutter's Point," he said.

"Thank God," I said.

"Don't thank God," he said. "Thank me."

Portis's Ranger was snow-buried, but parked right where he said it would be. He hurried ahead, tossed his snowshoes in the truck bed, and snapped his rifle into the rack on the rear window. He wiped the piled snow from the driver's-side door, then climbed inside to start her up. I stood and listened as the engine heaved and wheezed and I swear I didn't draw a breath until it finally caught and turned over. Then Portis jumped out and waved me over.

"Never a doubt," he said, and went to work the windows with his ice scraper.

He cleared my side first and told me the heat was pumping. I got in the truck with Jenna, but left the door open to ask him if he wanted me to drive. I knew it would piss him off but it had to be said. If nothing else, I had to try.

He stopped scraping and looked at me and shook his head.

"Shit," he said.

"I'm just saying," I said. "You've been drinking."

"You want to ride in this truck at all, I would suggest you shut up and sit in the passenger seat with that baby."

"It was just a question," I said.

"And I have given you an answer," he said, and kicked my door shut.

Portis chipped ice and when the air turned warm I held Jenna close to the vents to soak up the heat. I was worried Portis was pissed for real, which might affect his driving, but then he dropped to one knee and played some air guitar with the scraper. I couldn't help but bust out laughing. He was as glad as I was to be getting the hell out of the north hills. To finally get Jenna to safety.

"Crazy ass," I said, when he got in.

"Yeah," he said. "Maybe that's right."

"This heat feels good."

"You ain't kidding," he said.

"How far to the main road?"

"Not very," he said, and dropped the truck into gear.

We pushed through the snow and I was surprised by how little drift there was. I was going to ask Portis about it, but realized it would only lead to a lecture on how his keen instinct and knowledge of the hills had directed him to park exactly where he had. How he'd had the foresight not to bury himself beneath a foot of snow by parking on a slope.

In truth, Portis probably had no idea the truck was going to clear the trail until the second we pushed onto Grain Road in a spray of powder. I couldn't have cared less. We were out of the goddamn woods. I was so happy I decided not to mention the swell of heat I felt on Jenna's forehead, and the way it flashed against my palm like fever.

Chapter Ten

Shelton didn't know how long he slept on the floor with Kayla, but he woke in a panic for having slept at all. He looked outside and the sky was still gray above Jackson Lake, but it was no longer snowing. He'd lost precious time and didn't even bother to slip Kayla another V before heading out. He just took a piss and hurried for the truck with his nitrous tank and party balloons.

He started his Silverado and then cleared the windshield with a push broom he had on the porch. The truck was parked in a little rut and when he got back in the cab he started to rock her out. He tapped the gas and shifted into reverse, then tapped the gas and shifted forward. Gas, reverse. Gas, forward. Gas, reverse, and he was out! It was an art form, really.

He crossed the lake and then took Grain Road out of the hills to Highway 31, where he turned toward town and drove along

Lake Michigan, his Silverado swaying a little in the wind off the bay.

He wished it were somebody else that had crossed him and stole Jenna. Anybody but Little Hector. Shelton thought he had a good relationship with the Mexicans, and particularly the hard-working Hector Valquez. Hector was a good kid, and he had reliably moved Shelton's methamphetamines to his friends and family, his *familia*, by the quarter gram.

Frankly, Shelton preferred Hector to the spoiled shitty white kids he sometimes had occasion to work with. Hector didn't complain, didn't peddle as much in excuses. And even as mad as Shelton was, as violently angry as he felt, he knew that beneath that rage was no small amount of hurt. He'd trusted the little spic, and he was not above suffering the pain of that betrayal.

He passed the cement plant, still in the throes of its theatrical decay along the shore, and Shoreline Estates, the trailer park home of his youth. Then the highway bent around town and he could see the sleepy downtown and the steeple of the Methodist church. He could see the softly lit homes on the snowy streets and remembered when they had everything decked out for Christmas and Cutler looked like a little train-set village in the snow.

But he was not headed for the quaint part of town. Shelton was headed a little farther south, where the highway hit Detroit Street and ran smack into East Cutler.

East Cutler had always been the wrong side of the tracks, a small-town slum with the good sense to remain in a state of despair and impoverished shame until the Mexicans moved in and scared everybody shitless with their willingness to work. Even the criminal among them seemed poised for ascent.

Hector himself was using his drug money to pay for a few classes at the community college. Hector was after an Associate's in Business, whatever that was, and Shelton had sort of considered him an inspiration until he broke into his house and stole Jenna.

Hector lived on the corner of Detroit and Emmett Street, and Shelton pulled over on the curb a half block from his front stoop. Shelton shut his lights off and let the truck idle as the neighborhood spread out leaden gray around him. Four blocks of deteriorating row houses and everything was buttoned up and still, darker somehow than even the sky. Shelton noticed there wasn't a single light on around him and figured a transformer must have blown. Transformers in East Cutler always gave out in a storm, and sometimes for no reason at all. Nobody cared, except for the Mexicans.

Shelton had a balloon and peered out the windshield. He watched Hector's front door and wondered, should he wait a minute to see if the boy came out, or just bust right in and start breaking shit?

It was strange, but for a moment Shelton pined for the summer. He loved East Cutler in the warm weather, when the kids kicked soccer balls in the street and the men drank cold beers, *cervezas*, as they stood worrying over the hoods of their Chevrolets. In the summer in East Cutler the women hung laundry from their tiny balconies and stereos blared festive Mexican music. You could smell the grilled meat and the malt liquor and hear the chants of the girls skipping rope.

Shelton felt a little lonely then, thinking about the Mexican families inside their shabby homes, all snuggled up and cozy in the storm. He watched smoke rise from the slanted, weathered roofs and wondered what everybody was doing to pass the time. You could fit a shitload of Mexicans inside those itty-bitty row houses and he imagined whole families gathered around the hearth, making colorful quilts and boiling beans in oversized pots.

Shelton admired much about the Mexican culture, if he sat down to think about it. Mexicans stuck together and valued the extended family. They had a variety of uses for turquoise, which was a beautiful stone, if you wanted Shelton's opinion. They had also invented the tortilla and had many interesting tales of ancestral suffering. Mexicans were great workers and seemed generally trustworthy, which made this slave trade business all the more disheartening.

Shelton did a blue balloon, then a red one. Red and blue make purple so he did one of those in the name of symmetry. *Wha-wha-wha.*

He put his helmet on and plucked the Glock from his beltline. He figured he was going to have to go in and root the little fucker out. He couldn't just sit there all day and wait. Shelton knew how critical the first forty-eight were in the case of a missing person, but as soon as he opened the door he looked up to see Little Hector trotting down the front steps.

He flipped up his visor to be certain, but it was Little Hector all right. Shelton would recognize those baggy jeans and that dirty Dallas Cowboys coat anywhere. The boy fished a cigarette from his coat pocket and Shelton engaged the laser sight and held the red dot between Hector's jet-black eyebrows and waited for him to notice.

The plan was to freeze the boy where he stood. Keep him still with the laser and then walk up and come across his nose with the butt end of the Glock. Once Little Hector felt the blood rush, once that hard bone and cartilage had turned to sand, he'd be ready to talk. Wouldn't be no need for clever negotiations.

Hector lit his smoke, then looked up and saw the laser. And that fancy sight paid for itself with the slack-jawed terror with which Hector traced the red beam back to its source.

"That's right, motherfucker," Shelton said, and stepped toward him.

Hector shocked him then by pivoting hard to the left and running. It was perhaps the most amazing thing Shelton had ever witnessed, like a miracle or a stigmata. Hector had directly defied him and his Glock, and Shelton was so surprised he stood there for a minute with his *Tron* laser pinned to the snowbank where the boy had just been standing. Shelton didn't even think to turn and retake his aim until Hector had disappeared down an alley.

Shelton knew better than to try and catch him on foot. He tucked the Glock away and hopped back in the truck. He jammed the Silverado into drive and sped away from the curb. His tires squealed and spat snow.

He looked for Hector in the alleys and the gaps between row houses, but the little fucker had vanished. Shelton didn't suppose he got across the Rio Grande by being an easy target.

The mystery of Jenna's disappearance had been solved, though. If Hector wasn't involved, why would he take off running? He was knee deep in it. He had to be, to risk life and limb by running from Shelton and his magical red beam.

Shelton turned down a snow-narrowed alley at the end of the street. He took out a few trash cans and snapped his rearview back while the Silverado trailed paint. He pushed down harder on the gas and sparks flew off the brick until the whole alley seemed swarmed with glow bugs.

He barreled onto Jupiter Road and there was Hector, two blocks ahead and running hard through the drifted sidewalks. Shelton didn't know if he'd ever seen somebody run so fast. Hector was probably in a pair of Kmart high-tops, two sizes too small. Yet there he was, a low-flying flash of Mexican lightning.

Shelton punched the gas and covered some ground. Hector looked behind him, and when he saw Shelton gaining he rounded the next corner and nearly lost his footing, probably would have gone ass over elbows had he not grabbed a stop sign and flung himself forward onto Gibbons Street. Shelton skidded through the four-way himself and had to straighten the truck in the intersection.

Gibbons was a wide road, lined with discount storefronts and gas stations. It was Cutler's half-mile stretch of suburban sprawl, and Shelton drove it at the speed limit. There were always cops on Gibbons, and while Shelton's caution allowed Hector to regain his advantage, he was content to trail him as long as Hector was in his sights.

Shelton couldn't believe the way Hector kept running, the way he maintained his speed. If Shelton had to run as far as Hector he would have already keeled over and died twice. Shelton admired the boy's grit, which only made their quickly disintegrating friendship all the more difficult to bear.

Hector leapt the fence at the Saint Francis School playground while Shelton came to a stop at the red on the corner of Gibbons and Michigan. There he checked the glove box to see if he had any goodies stashed. He found a pint of whiskey, which was a relief.

He looked for something good on the radio, but it was all commercials. He glanced in the rearview, checked that he was all clear, and hoisted the pint for a swallow. He tapped the steering wheel and waited. There was nobody out, not even in this little ebb in the storm, so he decided to ignore the red and drive right on through. He had another gulp of whiskey, to keep the good times rolling.

Something was playing on the radio, but he didn't know what it was. He recognized the tune, though, and hummed along. He passed the Amoco Station and the Urgent Care and the comic-book store. He turned off on Stanley Street and there was Hector, finally slowed to a jog on the sidewalk.

He hoped he didn't have to kill Hector to get Jenna back, or even hurt him too badly, but that was really more of Hector's decision, wasn't it? That part didn't have a thing to do with Shelton. Hector would either cooperate or he wouldn't.

Meanwhile, the little absconder had run himself into a bit of a predicament. It turned out there weren't any side alleys or sharp corners on Stanley Street. There was just the road and the razor wire where Stanley's Used Ford stretched for blocks. Little Hector had trapped himself on a straightaway and Shelton had him dead to rights.

He didn't guess Hector would stop and try to climb that fence, not when all Shelton would have to do is get out and tackle his ass to the ground. Or maybe shoot him in the back of the knee, but only as a warning and proof of the seriousness of his intent.

At the end of the street was the bike path that ran along the Bear River, which was obviously why Hector had chosen this route. Hit the bike path and he'd be safe, relatively. Shelton couldn't drive farther than the turnaround at the end of the street, and even as tired as Hector was there was no way Shelton could catch him by foot.

The boy's plan had been foiled, though. Shelton had caught him long before the turnaround, and he slowed the Silverado to a roll, then parked along the curb. He was no more than five feet behind Hector now, and he gave the horn a couple quick taps in greeting. Wisely, Hector stopped running and turned to face him.

Shelton put the truck in park, then opened the door and stepped onto the sidewalk. He pointed the Glock and put the laser square on the boy's chest. Shelton thought about how precarious it all was, life and the universe.

Chapter Eleven

Portis drove the center of Grain Road and the Ranger held a hard, straight line through the drifted shoulders. The pines were set close and the snow had started to fall again.

Somebody was on the radio, singing about the Houston sky and galloping through bluebonnets. Portis had his window cracked and he smoked as he drove. He nodded at the stereo and said it was Warren Zevon.

"Who is that?"

It was a question I immediately regretted as Portis cast a grieving look in my direction.

"Clearly I have failed you," he said. "Clearly I did not do enough to teach you what was important when I had the chance."

"Whatever," I said. "Who was the third president of the United States?"

"Thomas Jefferson," he said. "Who was the fifth?"

"I forgot you knew the presidents," I said.

"That's only part of what I know," he said. "And James Monroe was the fifth president of the United States."

"Just pay attention," I said. "I can barely tell where the road is."

"And you wanted to drive."

Portis leaned forward to wipe at some fog on the windshield and I could see that he was in the height of his glory. He had a smug half smile and clearly believed some critical victory had been won against me. I shook my head at Jenna.

"Don't mind your uncle Portis," I said. "He's just old and sour at the world."

"For your information," he said. "Warren Zevon is only one of the greatest American songwriters of all time. In spite of the fact that the Rock and Roll Hall of Fame has yet to recognize his brilliance. But yet Madonna is enshrined there. As is ABBA."

"Madonna was a bad-ass," I said.

"Madonna tongued-kissed a black Jesus," said Portis. "For which I credit her."

"What?"

"Forget it," he said. "Before your time. The point is, they can induct whoever they want into their ridiculous club, but do not expect me to take you seriously as an institution when you deny artists of Warren's stature in favor of a disco scourge like Barry Gibb."

I wanted to say something about the road in front of us, how more and more I couldn't tell it from the shoulder. I wanted Portis to slow down, but feared angering him in earnest, which would only lead him to hammer the gas to spite me.

I held Jenna tight and wondered if it would be better or worse for her if I strapped myself in with a belt. The belt would protect me, but if there was an accident I worried the strap would strangle her.

I thought the best thing was to put the lap belt on and slip the shoulder strap behind me. I did so quickly, worried my precautions would offend Portis.

"He wrote a song called 'Keep Me in Your Heart,' " Portis said. "It was right before he died of cancer. And I will tell you right now that song will hollow you out with its truth. You will feel as if a piece of your own heart has been carved away. And what did Barry Gibb do? Wore tight pants and made music for homosexuals, that's what."

I did not know what there was to say about Warren Zevon or Barry Gibb. I didn't suppose there was anything I could say. I was just glad Portis had the wherewithal to issue such a rant without slurring. That was really the time to worry about Portis, when he started shaving the edges off his syllables and his words turned rounded and lazy and all slid together in a stew.

I held Jenna and let myself think of what I might do when we cleared the hills. We would take Jenna to the hospital, of course. Then I might grab that hot meal with Portis after all. Lunch at the Elias Brothers sounded pretty good, though what I really wanted was a shower and some sleep. I couldn't wait to blast off the cold and the filth and then crawl beneath some heavy blankets and close my eyes. I would sleep for as long as I wanted, for as long as I could, and then I would wake and return for Carletta.

I had told Portis earlier I'd never come back to the hills, but even as I said it I knew it was a lie. I needed some rest, but I was no more comfortable leaving Mama than I was when I drove up Grain Road the night before.

I looked out at the Three Fingers and it was frozen where it cut through the pines and pooled. I thought about the white water down the hill and wondered how far north we were of Shelton's. I was going to say something about it to Portis, about how far we'd come, when I felt the Ranger drop.

It was a bunny hop, really, the brief sense that we were falling before the truck hit the snow and we were pushed forward in our seats. I turned my shoulder toward the dash and smacked it hard, but I kept Jenna from the impact as best I could.

I bit down hard on my tongue and after the truck settled some from the jarring my mouth filled with blood and Jenna started to cry.

"Shit," Portis said, and tapped the gas.

I could hear the tires spin and Portis put it in reverse, but the truck wouldn't budge. I spit some blood on the floor and then looked over at him behind the wheel.

"We're stuck," he said.

The headlights were cast toward a small stand of birch, and between them and the trees there was deep, drifted snow. Portis tapped the gas and tried to rock us out again. He went from forward to reverse, then back to forward, but the tires only spun.

"I drove us off the road," he said.

"I could get out and push," I said.

Portis reached out and punched off the radio.

"Hush," he said.

He rolled his window down and we were blasted by the wind. I bounced Jenna on my knee to try and calm her. It took me a moment, but then I heard the buzzing.

"Shit," I said. "Is that them?"

Portis leapt from the truck and told me to grab Jenna's things. I threw the bag over my shoulder and pushed the door open as Jenna's crying reached full throat.

"They're close," he said.

I nearly fell forward when I hit the ground but I plunged a hand into the snow to keep from going over. The drift was to my shins and I stumbled again when I tried to step forward. Then I felt Portis behind me, grabbing me by the hood to pull me free.

He pointed at a stand of jack pines and said there was a deer blind at the top of the rise just beyond them. The whole hillside was a dull, gray blur to me, but Portis knew every inch and read that little spread of trees like a neon sign. He took off with his own rucksack and the rifle and I followed with both hands cupped beneath Jenna to keep her head from bouncing.

I could hear the sleds nearing but I was afraid to turn around and look. I ran hard and straight and nearly slammed into the blind before Portis swung the door open and guided me in. I'd been looking in the trees and never thought he meant a ground blind.

It was a small square of old, weather-beaten wood and there were openings cut in on two sides for shooting. The ground was dirt and snow-dusted grass, and I fell back on my butt and looked to Portis. He told me to fix Jenna a bottle.

"Keep her quiet," he said. "Cover her mouth if you have to."

I dug through the backpack but could not find the formula. Jenna was shrieking and Portis turned to me as he pulled a box of bullets from the ruck and loaded the rifle.

"Cover her up," he said.

I put my hand over Jenna's mouth and forced myself to squeeze. I could feel her lips quivering and trailing spit along my palm and when she began to kick I pulled back and her cries spilled out.

Portis squatted beneath the window and pointed at the corner of the blind directly across from him. I slid over with Jenna and backed myself against the wall while he eased up to look through the window.

"They seen us," he said.

"Shelton?"

"No," he said. "It looks like Arrow and Krebs."

"Is it just the two?"

"Yeah. Looks like. They don't see the blind yet, but they seen the truck. Probably heard us too."

I jostled Jenna in my arms.

"I'm not running," I whispered.

"You run if I tell you run."

"We'll see if I do," I said.

Portis aimed the rifle through the window and steadied it on his shoulder. He asked me if I could see out, and I sat up into a squat so that I could.

"On the right is Arrow," he said. "The other is Krebs."

They were both moving in a slow crouch. Krebs had a handgun drawn in the center of the hill, while Arrow carried a pack strapped to his shoulders and moved up the tree line.

"I got a sight on either one of you," Portis called. "And I don't mind shooting. Just so we're all on the same page."

Krebs froze and then dropped into the snow while Arrow stooped lower, came a few more yards up the hill, and took cover in the pines.

"Here comes the warning," Portis said, and fired off into the trees.

The men ducked low and Jenna nearly leapt out of my lap. She cried out again and I whispered to her that it was okay. That everything was going to be fine.

It was Krebs that hollered up the hill.

"Who you got in that blind with you, Portis?"

"That is not your concern."

"I think you got a little baby up there with you. And Arrow said he seen a girl."

"Well, Arrow can't see for shit."

"Baby don't sound too happy," said Arrow. "From the way it's crying."

"She senses your presence and it does not agree with her."

"What's funny," Krebs said, "is we had a baby go missing last night. Down at the farmhouse. And Rick put out a reward. Five thousand dollars to whoever brings her back."

"Five thousand," Portis said. "That ain't much for a baby. Is it white?"

"Far as I know," said Krebs.

"If it's white it should be worth ten. Old Rick's playing you for suckers, boys. A white baby is worth its weight in gold. Did you know that all around the world, people prefer the white baby to other races? Were you aware of that, Krebs? People will take a white baby over a member of their own tribe. I think that's sad, don't you?"

"You know," Krebs said. "It turns out I don't have time for your bullshit."

"Is that right?" Portis said. "Then why you still out there in the snow?"

"Because we intend to take this baby back to its rightful mother."

"You don't know nothing about it," Portis said. "This baby was in a state of neglect."

"If you were smart on this we could see about a share of the profit for you," said Krebs. "A little pinch, anyway."

"The baby will stay with me," Portis said. "There is nothing to negotiate."

"You're going to give that baby up," Arrow said. "Or I will gas you out of the blind."

Arrow had slid off his pack and assumed a catcher's crouch behind the tree. He was gangly, stoop-shouldered, and a member of the McGraws—a loathsome Cutler family with militia ties. He had on a camouflage parka and ski mask and held up a cylinder for us to see. It was roughly the size of a soda can and he withdrew it quickly.

"It's a little homemade mix," he said. "You might call it tear gas. At least that's what it most closely resembles in terms of overall effect."

"Portis," Krebs shouted, and raised his hands to the sky. "May I have a word with my associate, please?"

"You may stand there and speak to this imbecile if you like, but you will not be taking a single step in any direction."

"Fine," Krebs said, then turned to Arrow and called out across the hill.

"What the hell are you doing, Arrow?" Krebs said.

"I'm going to smoke them out," Arrow said. "Then we will charge Portis. He will be blinded and we will tackle him easily and then get the girl and the baby. You will do your part, Krebs. You will charge or you are not entitled to an even split of the money."

"You can't gas the baby," Krebs said.

"Portis is the target here, not the baby."

"Yes," Krebs said. "But the baby is in the fucking blind with him!"

"Baby or no, I'm not going to sit here all day and let him take potshots at us."

"That's a can of chicken noodle soup," Portis shouted.

"Try me and see."

"He's gone rogue on this," Krebs said. "Portis, I don't know what he's got in that can."

"I'm counting down from ten," Arrow shouted.

"Arrow!" Krebs shouted.

"Back off, Krebs. I'm going to flush them from that blind and if Portis leaves the baby in there to breathe the gas then it is his own fault. Nine!"

"Goddamn it," Krebs shouted. "Just come out with that baby, Portis!"

"He's bluffing," Portis said.

"I don't think he is," Krebs said, and retook his cover in the snow.

"I'm not bluffing one bit," Arrow said. "Eight!"

Portis looked at me and then at Jenna.

"Is that really gas?" I whispered.

"I suspect," he said. "He's a regular Einstein with them gases. Probably came out on this venture based solely on the possibility that he might get to let off one of his prized grenades."

"What if he's bluffing, though?"

"It's not our bluff to call. Not with Jenna sitting right there in your lap."

"Seven!" Arrow shouted.

"I can't believe I drove us off the goddamn road," said Portis.

"It's not your fault," I said.

"I am sorry I could not get you off this hill."

"It's nobody's fault," I said.

"Nobody but Shelton Potter's," he said. "And the two stooges out there."

"Six!"

"This is on you, Portis!" Krebs shouted. "This goes any further, it's on you. Just walk out of the fucking blind already!"

Portis looked at me and shook his head. I was crying but I told him it was okay.

"Go ahead," I said. "We have to."

I stood up with Jenna, and as Portis went to make his concession I saw a flicker of light in the woods. The wind pushed west and then there was a sucking sound, a sudden *whoosh*—like a vacuum on thick carpet—and I swear I felt the heat all the way up in the blind.

Arrow never even screamed. There was only the hiss and pop of the flames as he ran onto the open hillside, the blackened, flailing core at the center of a ball of fire. He was like a comet streaking across cold sky until he stopped and was wholly consumed—a felled star on the white snow burning.

Portis waved at me to stay down and he put the rifle on Krebs, who had stood up and was slack-jawed staring.

"My God," said Krebs.

"Easy now," Portis said. "I got the rifle on your chest."

"He lit it," Krebs said. "Then burst straight into fire."

"The fucker only got to five," Portis said.

"He was going for the element of surprise," Krebs said.

"He was going to gas this baby," Portis said.

"He went up like a Roman candle," said Krebs.

"It was an end he has long been destined for."

"I've never seen anything like it," said Krebs.

"I am fine with it," Portis said. "I have never liked him one bit."

"What the hell was in that can?"

"I don't know," Portis said. "But you're lucky the wind is blowing the other way."

"I am going to cut my losses and go back down this hill," Krebs said. "Do not shoot."

"I won't shoot," Portis said. "Because you're going to help us push that truck out."

"Fine," Krebs said. "But then I am through with this mess."

I was still huddled with Jenna in the corner of the blind and put my back to the window to shield her some from the cold.

"Should I come?" I said.

"Don't yet," Portis said. "Let that smoke clear a bit and then come down. Give us five minutes."

Jenna was still crying, but softer now. Portis finally set his rifle down and drank from his whiskey.

"Did you see it?" he said.

"Most of it," I said. "I think."

"You should try to forget the image," he said.

"I don't think that's likely."

"I have never seen a thing like it in my life," he said.

"I don't smell anything," I said.

"I don't either," he said. "Perhaps he absorbed all of his brew into his own skin, like a sponge. Maybe that's why he went up like that. So quick."

"It only took a second," I said.

"I am not a scientist," Portis said. "And I am glad to say that I do not understand the physics of what just happened."

He took another knock of whiskey, then took the bottle and the rifle and stepped outside. He whistled as he stared at the fire, already diminishing in the snow. I closed my eyes and breathed.

"The flaming Arrow," he said.

I did not grieve the death of Arrow McGraw. It shocked and upset me, but when it was contrasted to the idea of handing Jenna over

I viewed it more favorably. I was also comforted by the fact that he had done it to himself, that while upbringing and genetic code could not be entirely ignored, in the end it was Arrow himself that lit the fuse.

It is a terrible thing to see a man burn down in front of you, but you would be surprised by the things you can walk through when it is necessary to keep walking. Besides, I had Jenna to attend to. Her face was blushed red and now there was real heat on her forehead when I put my cold palm against it.

I waited for what seemed like five minutes, then hurried down the hill with my gaze held straight ahead. I was not interested in glimpsing whatever remained of Arrow, and kept my focus on Jenna—who hadn't done a thing wrong in the entirety of her existence, who hadn't asked for any of the insanity that surrounded her.

I heard the rumble of Krebs's sled, but he was already out of sight and the truck was still submerged when we got to the base of the hill. I could not see Portis, but when I called out for him he answered with a grunt from behind the truck.

I hurried to find him on his hands and knees. He was bleeding from the stomach and trying to crawl forward, but he gave up when he saw me and slumped against the rear tire.

"Portis!" I shouted.

"He shot me," he said. "He didn't even mean to, which I think makes it worse. I was kicking some snow away from the tires when he came back to help. He was walking with that pistol swinging and then he dropped into the snow where it falls off and shot me on accident."

Portis looked at one of his blood-streaked hands, then replaced it over the wound in his stomach and groaned.

"That fucking idiot," he said, and knocked his head against the tire.

"You're bleeding bad," I said.

"He was more afraid than I was. He shot me and then I sat here and watched him piss in his pants. When that was over he got on the sled and took off back down the trail."

"Do you think he went for help?"

"Krebs?" Portis said. "Hell no. He's on probation and probably high as a kite to boot. He's beelining it for home. That fucker will be in Canada by nightfall."

Portis reached for his whiskey and had a long slug. He emptied the bottle and then threw it off into the snow.

"People will reveal themselves to you, Percy," he said. "In single moments they will show you what they are, and Krebs is exactly the coward I have always suspected."

I leaned closer and told Portis he was going to be fine. I said he just needed to try and get up. I said all he had to do was put one foot in front of the other and walk.

Jenna was hollering and I must have been talking a streak because Portis finally waved at me to shut up. He told me to concentrate on the baby.

"You got to try and calm that baby down," he said.

"We got to get you out of here," I said.

"I ain't going anywhere," he said.

"Portis," I said. "Please."

"You done good," he said. "And I'm proud of you."

"Don't be proud," I said. "Just get up."

"Go fix that baby a bottle," he said. "Then light me a cigarette and bring me my whiskey. There should be a pint stashed beneath the driver's seat."

I did what Portis said. I mixed the bottle in the cab, though I spilled most of the formula with my shaking hands. Then I got the whiskey and the cigarette. I sat beside Portis with Jenna in my lap and put the cigarette between his lips. I opened the whiskey and handed him the bottle.

"Where's the baby?" he said.

"She's right here," I said. "She's in the papoose."

"She's calming."

"She's okay," I said, and looked down at her.

"You're good girls," he said. "The both of ya."

"Just try and get up for me, Portis. Please."

"Lighter is in my pocket," he said.

I lit the cigarette and he took a few deep draws before I pulled it out and let him exhale. He coughed out the smoke and groaned from the pain. He drank some more whiskey and then called for the cigarette. I went to put it in his mouth but he reached out with his hand and smoked it himself.

"We didn't end right," he said. "Me and your mother. But we had some good times, didn't we? The four of us."

"We did," I said.

"You remember that time we went bowling out to Victories? When Starr kept slipping and falling on her butt?"

"I remember."

"You do?"

"I do."

"I don't believe you."

"She wouldn't put the shoes on," I said. "She liked some boy and she was convinced he was going to come in and see her in the clown shoes so she bowled in her socks instead."

Portis shook his head.

"She was boy crazy," he said. "Hormones, like *zow*."

He laughed, then gripped his belly and winced. I turned away when the bile came, but it clung to his beard when he coughed and stretched in a long line from the corner of his mouth. He swiped at it with his hands and I could feel the tears welling in my eyes.

"I think about them days sometimes," he said. "The old days, or whatever. I think about you girls."

"I think about it, too," I said.

"We had some good times," he said.

"We did," I said. "We had the best times."

"I ain't going to make it," he said.

"You've got to try."

"I'm going to die right here where I sit," he said.

"No, you are not," I said.

"Please don't argue with me," he said.

"I'm not going to let you die, Portis. That's not what's going to happen."

"I wouldn't bother with that rifle," he said. "Travel light and be smart. We bought you a little time but you got to stay off the road now. Get back in them woods."

"I'm not going anywhere," I said.

"Whiskey," he said.

I put the bottle to his lips and he took another gulp.

"There's an element of relief to it," he said. "There truly is."

"Just get up, Portis. Please."

"I'm not getting up. I can't."

"We need you," I said.

He turned off to the side and started to mutter. I made a fist and thumped him on the chest but he never turned back to face me. I kept pounding and then I grabbed at his coat and tried to pull him toward me, almost like I thought I could yank him back somehow—like death is just some edge you can keep someone from falling off.

Portis didn't come back, of course. He was gone and I screamed out as I watched the life leave his eyes—like the light going down on a dimmer switch.

Chapter Twelve

Shelton had just put the gun on Hector when the buzzing in his chest began. He thought he was having some sort of indigestion, or perhaps a heart attack, until he heard the ringing and realized it was the cell.

He took the phone from the front pocket of his snowsuit and kept the laser sight on the boy. They were far enough away from the bike path, two blocks at least, so Shelton wasn't worried about Hector slipping away again. He was perfectly happy to keep the boy frozen there for another minute or two while he took his call. First and foremost, Shelton was a businessman.

It was Krebs. Krebs never bothered to say hello, or ask Shelton how he was. He just launched right into his story about how Arrow had been burned to a crisp.

"Do what?" Shelton said.

"He's burned up," said Krebs. "He's dead."

"You say Arrow McGraw has been burned up dead?"

"That's what I said."

"Goodness," said Shelton.

"We found that goddamn baby. Portis had her in a fucking deer blind. We could hear it crying."

"You found the baby?"

"Yeah," he said. "And then Arrow set himself on fire."

"Why did he do that?"

"What do you mean, why? It was a goddamn accident."

"Did you get her? Did you get Jenna?"

"Hell no," he said.

"Why not?"

"Because Arrow burned and then I run."

"What did you run for?"

" 'Cause Portis had a rifle! He had the position in that blind, too. Wasn't nothing I could do."

"So what you're saying is that Portis Dale has the baby?"

"That's what I'm saying."

"So this doesn't have nothing to do with Little Hector or the Mexicans?"

"There weren't no Mexicans. I don't know nothing about no Mexicans."

"Thank God."

"Yeah, thank God Arrow didn't get killed by a Mexican. That would have made all the difference, you fucking dipshit."

"It's not like that," Shelton said. "It's complicated."

"Not for Arrow."

"Arrow's dead," Shelton said.

"I know, motherfucker. I'm the one that called and told you."

"What now?" Shelton said.

"Now?" said Krebs. "Now nothing. Now, I'm going home. Clemens is still out there somewhere though. That sonofabitch is hell bent on that five thousand dollars. He told me he planned to shoot Portis Dale dead if need be. Thing is, I borrowed that sonofabitch my little six-shooter last week."

"You're saying Clemens is still out there looking? And that he intends to shoot Portis Dale if need be?"

"With my gun," Krebs said.

"Well," said Shelton. "That sounds like a plan."

"It ain't no plan," he said. "You fucking moron. You ain't never had a plan in your life and this whole thing is so fucked I'm going to go home and spend the rest of the night wishing I'd never met your stupid ass."

Krebs hung up the phone and Shelton was not unbothered by his tone and accusations. Krebs had a right to be upset, that much was true, but his anger had seemed a touch excessive, a bit too personal in nature, if you wanted Shelton's opinion.

Shelton let his own gun fall to his side. Little Hector looked at him for a moment, his eyes wide and unblinking. Poor bastard, Shelton thought.

"Go on home then," he said.

The boy turned and ran and Shelton watched him until he reached the path at the end of the road, until he disappeared into the smudge of trees Shelton could see through the gently falling snow. He was relieved he did not have to kill Hector after all, and hoped they might remain friends when all this was over.

Shelton got back in the truck and gassed himself a balloon. It was time to refocus. Arrow was dead, but Shelton didn't have any ideas about what to do about that fact. Clemens was still out on the prowl but he was damn near sixty years old and on his second hip. So Shelton wasn't exactly sure what the next move was. Times like these made him doubt his abilities as a leader. He did a balloon, and then another. His head went *wha-wha-wha*.

He put the truck back in gear and all of a sudden recognized the song playing on the radio. It was the one about a rocket man, and being gone a long, long time.

Shelton flipped his blinker on and made the turn back onto Gibbons Road. The clouds had dropped again and the gray sky had gone bright with snow. Revelation indeed, Shelton thought. If there was any doubt before there could be none now. This was a blizzard with the feel of biblical retribution.

Shelton was headed for the highway and then the north hills. It was time to find Portis Dale and the baby. Little Jenna had been gone long enough. He hummed along with the radio and reached for the pint bottle. He drove through the quiet streets in the storm.

Chapter Thirteen

I do not remember leaving Portis at the truck. I do not remember anything after the moment he died but a sound like a jet engine rising from the base of my brain and growing louder and louder until I was drowned inside of myself by the roaring.

I suppose I picked up Jenna and walked away, because the first thing I remember is being back in the woods and the baby crying. I did not try to comfort her because she was hungry and I had left the water in Portis's truck. I hadn't had the wherewithal to grab it, and who knows how much distance I'd already put between us and that hillside.

I realized too that I was on the wrong side of the river. I had thought I was east of the Three Fingers and had planned to walk south back to the shanty, but the woods were too thin around me and the snow was falling hard through the gaps. I was walking in the open and the clouds helped my cover some but there was no quarter from the cold.

After a time I came to a woodpile, stacked between two birch and covered with a tarp. Beyond the woodpile was a trailer where I could hear a screen door swing on its hinges. The snow in the yard was drifted and there were no lights in the trailer as I came closer.

The forest was thin but the trees around me reached high and I could hear the branches rattle as the wind pushed through. Jenna was awake and she was fussy—thrashing in the papoose and kicking.

"One minute, sweetness," I said. "And we're going to get you inside."

The trailer was one of Shelton's. I knew he had a couple stashed in the hills, single-wides he used for cooking, and we were going to have to take our chances and go inside. There were no cars or sleds parked out front, and though I believed we were near the farmhouse I didn't think it likely Shelton would have walked through the storm. I thought the trailer was probably empty and it was the best chance we had to find some water and some warmth.

I went to the back porch, caught the screen when it swung, and pinned it to the wall with my hand. I looked in through a panel window but it was pitch black inside and when I tried the door it was locked. I stepped back, let go of the screen for one second, and it swung loose and smacked me on the back of the head.

I screamed and stumbled off the porch. There was a throb at

the top of my skull and it widened until it filled my nostrils and pushed up hard against the back of my eyeballs. I took a moment to gather myself and then spat at the snow. As I might have mentioned, it starts to seem personal.

I went for the woodpile next, grabbed a log, and propped it beneath a small window on the other end of the trailer. I stepped up and my face was level with the glass. Jenna was crying now and I turned to the side to protect her as I brushed away the snow and came to the crusted ice beneath.

I could not see through the window but I uncurled my fists and put my hands to its sides and pushed. I pushed until the freeze crackled and fell away from the seams and the window rose in its frame.

I stepped down to take off the pack. I got the formula and put it on the windowsill, then slid Jenna's bottle in the pocket of my hoodie.

"Almost there now," I said.

I peered inside with the flashlight and I could see a rust-stained tub and a sink and toilet. There was a drip coming from the ceiling and it plunked loudly in that small, tinny room. Finally, I took off the papoose with Jenna inside and tried to lower her into the sink. She cried out and reached for me and I snapped her back up.

"I know, baby girl," I said. "It's just for a minute."

She cried harder the second time and in the end I had to force her into the sink. I came in next, dropping a few feet to the floor, where I reached for the formula and pulled the window shut behind me. Then I went for Jenna.

It was warm in the bathroom. There was heat pulsing through

the register, but that didn't worry me. I came back to the fact that there were no vehicles outside and figured Shelton must have forgot to flip the switch when he last left. I turned my flashlight toward the darkened hall and there was insulation falling from the ceiling tiles and trash strewn across the carpet. Typical Shelton. An empty trailer full of toxic waste, and he was pumping it with hot air.

There was water, too, and when I cranked the sink handle it sprang fast and hot from the faucet. I filled the bottle, mixed in the formula, and fed Jenna on the floor.

I leaned back against the tub as feeling hit my fingers like small flames at the ends of match tips. It felt good to have the papoose off, to let the muscles in my back uncoil.

"Eat, baby girl," I said. "Eat."

Jenna sucked down her bottle and then her breath came slow and steady. I knew she was going to fall asleep and that brought me comfort. I wanted to set her down, but mostly I was glad for our tiny, predictable pattern. She would eat and then she would sleep, and I was glad to have something the both of us could depend on.

I put her down in the papoose after she fell off and let her sleep on the tile. The formula was nearly empty when I filled the scoop; there was nothing left but a little pinch in the corner of the canister and that wouldn't make us so much as a gulp. I hoped she gathered whatever rest she could now, because she'd be running on empty from here on in.

I walked into the hall with the flashlight and pushed through the trash. I was looking for a phone but there was only more filth.

Emptied bottles of drain cleaner and lighter fluid, smoked soda bottles and tubing and black bubbles burned into the carpet.

I walked from one end of the trailer clear to the other and it was there in the hall between a bedroom and a storage closet that I found Carletta facedown on the floor.

Her left arm was twisted and tucked beneath her stomach and both legs splayed behind her in a V. She wasn't dead. I could see her shoulders rise with breath and when I rolled her over she groaned and looked up. She was alive but her eyes were as flat and still as stones.

"It's me," I said. "Mama. It's Percy."

"Sweetgirl," she whispered, and reached for me.

The thing that surprised me most was my own surprise. I couldn't believe I hadn't thought Mama might be there. The trailer was as logical a place as any for her to wait out the storm, and when she wasn't at the farmhouse I should have known she would have gone somewhere nearby to cook up a batch and gotten stranded. I should have known she would resurface at the moment Jenna needed me most, after I'd already lost Portis and nearly forgotten why I'd come to the hills in the first place.

I lifted her from the shoulders and pulled her close to my chest. Her arms had gone limp and her hair was grease-damp and clumped together in strings. She was in a tattered sweatshirt and blue jeans and smelled like burned shit. She looked like she'd been spit out by the storm itself.

"Mama," I said. "I'm right here."

Carletta cried in my arms, and when I cried back I couldn't be exactly sure why. I was wild with anger, but I was relieved too. Or at least I was so emptied out and exhausted that it felt like relief. Mama was alive and I was there to hold her.

"It's okay, Mama," I said. "I'm here now."

I backed against the wall for balance and pushed myself up with Carletta's arms draped around my shoulders. She was wobbly on her feet and she leaned hard against me. I told her she was doing great and steadied her against a hip. I put my arm around her waist and walked her down the hall.

"I'm so sorry," she said.

"It's okay," I said. "Everything is going to be okay, Mama."

We walked into the bathroom and I eased her down to the floor. She didn't say anything about Jenna, if she noticed her at all. Mama just hugged her arms close to her chest and sat staring at the rotting tile floor. She was mumbling something about the cold.

I set Jenna in the hall just outside the door and scanned the carpet around her for chemical spills or anything sharp. I checked the ceiling above for leaks and then gave her another glance. She was sleeping deeply. She was as sweet as she could be.

I went back to Mama, flipped the switch in the bathroom, and let the overhead blink on. It was yellowy and dim, and there was a buzzing in the bulb as it burned. Mama coughed and her chest rattled with phlegm.

"Let's get you cleaned up," I said.

I turned on the shower and the head sputtered and spat until the stream pushed through clean. I put my hand in to test the temperature and it was warm.

"I'm so cold," she said.

"The water's nice," I said.

I helped her pull off her sweatshirt and in the light I could see the purple crisscross of veins over her chest and arms and then the brownish, misshapen splotches on her neck and shoulders. Mama leaned forward to step out of her pants and when she saw the sides of her shit-streaked thighs she started to sob.

"I'm so sorry," she said, and held to the edge of the tub for balance.

"Let's just get you cleaned up," I said.

I guided her into the shower and asked if she had anything clean to wear. She stood shivering, arms wrapped around her shoulders as the water washed over.

"I've got a bag," she said. "There might be something in my bag."

"Where's your bag, Mama?"

"I don't know," she said, and cried harder. "I don't know where my bag is, sweetness. I'm sorry."

"It's okay," I said. "I'll go look."

The bag was in the bedroom and there were some clean enough clothes inside, but what gave me pause was the baby blanket I found in the end pocket.

The thing is, not all junkies are like you see in the movies. They're not always crashing cars and setting shit on fire. Sometimes it isn't all that dramatic. Mama, for instance, loved nothing more than to sit on the couch and knit while she got stoned. All winter long she'd been working on a blanket for my nephew, Tanner, and I couldn't believe she'd actually finished it.

I held it to my face and felt the softness of the yarn. It was baby blue and edged in red. Carletta had sized it a twin because she wanted to make something Tanner could grow into, and I will readily admit I never thought she'd see it through. That blanket was a scraggly square of yarn the last I saw, but it seemed she'd used her high in the hills to fuel a cross-stitch binge.

Starr might not have spoken to Mama since she moved to Portland, but I thought the blanket could be enough to get her to drop a card in the mail. Maybe a nice little thank-you note and a photo of Tanner to boot. I knew we might never be a family like you see on television, where everybody's tribulations bring them closer and make them stronger in the end—but I believed we could still be something. A blanket might not seem like much to most, but I swear it swelled my heart as I folded it in a square and left it beside the bag.

I found a dusty glass in the kitchen, ran some cool water, then returned to the bathroom to find Mama sitting in the tub, shivering. The shower was off and I handed her the glass and told her to drink.

"The water went cold," she said.

"That's okay," I said. "Go ahead and drink. Have a little bit, at least."

She forced a sip, then another. She gave the glass back, then pulled her legs up and circled her arms around her shins. Her teeth were chattering as she leaned forward and rested her head on her knees.

"I'm sorry," I said. "I don't think there's any towels."

"Oh," Carletta said, and her voice cracked hard. "Oh, sweet one."

I kneeled on the linoleum and reached into the tub and held her wet body against my own. Mama cried and I could feel the thump of each sob as it rang through her ribs. Mama's sadness was always physical like that—it was its own special type of violence.

"It's okay," I whispered. "I'm right here, Mama. Everything will be okay."

"Sweetgirl," she said, and stroked my hair.

"I saw you finished the blanket," I said. "For Tanner. It's beautiful."

Mama started to come in and out then, mumbling about how sorry she was and how things were going to be different from now on. She was dry enough to dress so I got her out of the tub and slid on her jeans. I pulled her sweatshirt on and was startled by a glaring sliver of scalp—a wide, bone-white shore between patches of hair.

I tried to help her to her feet. I wanted to get her to the couch in the living room, but Carletta begged me to let her go.

"Just let me sleep, baby," she said.

It might sound bad, but I quit struggling and set her down right there on the tile floor. If there was one skill Mama had it was sleeping anywhere her head dropped.

I left Mama and took Jenna down the hall to the bedroom, wrapped her in Tanner's blanket, and set her down on the carpet. She was burning up with fever but the blanket's fit was perfect and I thought it might help her to sweat it out. I sat down beside her and watched her breathe. I put my finger to her cheek and I started to cry. Portis was gone.

Chapter Fourteen

The first thing Shelton did when he returned to the farmhouse was tend to Kayla. He needed to keep her down, but decided to bypass the V and go a subtler, more gentle route.

He stopped at his secret drawer in the kitchen for a joint, then sat beside her on the floor and crossed his legs Indian style. He put his fingers to her pulse and felt the faint trace of a beat. He loved her, loved her so much it made his heart hurt, put an honest-to-God ache in his ribs.

The Talking Heads sang, *Check out Mr. Businessman . . . He bought some wild, wild life.*

Shelton lit the joint and took a drag, but it was only to generate some smoke to blow in Kayla's direction. So she might be warmed and comforted in her sleep. So if she woke to the waiting terror she might have the edges of it blunted, if only for a moment.

He turned her over on her back, ran a finger down her cheek, and then blew a line of smoke into her mouth with a kiss. He watched it expel through her nose, then she coughed and some trailed out that lovely part in her lips. He kissed her forehead and then heard the phone buzz. It was Clemens.

Shelton wasn't used to Rick's boys calling him up on the phone and the truth was he was a little flattered by all the attention. He picked up and Clemens was breathing hard on the other end.

"We got bodies up on this hill," he said. "Somebody burned to death. My money's on Arrow McGraw, and Portis Dale is lying dead at the bottom of the hill by his truck. He was gut shot and there ain't no baby."

"There's no baby?"

"Baby is gone."

"Where?"

"I don't know."

"Why don't you know?"

" 'Cause it was gone when I got here. Didn't leave no note."

"Portis is dead?"

"Stone cold."

"Did you shoot him?"

"No. I found him like this."

"Krebs said you planned to kill Portis Dale."

"I did not."

"Krebs said you borrowed his six-shooter and were ready to pull if needed."

"Well," said Clemens. "It sounds to me like we know who killed Portis."

"Fucker lied to me."

"Krebs is a piece of shit," Clemens said. "I've warned you about him before."

"So what happened to Jenna?"

"I don't hardly want to say."

"I think you should."

"I don't have any way of knowing really."

"You got to say it, Clemens. Whatever it is."

"I'm worried is all," Clemens said. "I started thinking like maybe that Wolfdog took the baby. Dragged it off and God knows what. Portis usually does have that Wolfdog with him."

"You think Wolfdog took the baby?"

"I think," Clemens said. "But I don't know."

"Jesus, Lord," said Shelton.

"I'm heading over right now," Clemens said.

"To where?"

"The farmhouse."

"For what?"

"We need to sit down and figure this thing through. We got dead bodies up here, Shelton. We can't just leave them out."

"I'm not home," Shelton said, and looked out his window at the raging snow.

"Where you at?"

"Charlevoix the Beautiful."

He supposed it was as good a place as any to pretend to be.

"Doing what?"

"Talking to some folks, might know something about this baby."

"There ain't nothing else to know. That baby is somewhere up in the hills."

"That's why you got to keep looking."

"I plan to," Clemens said. "But we've got to get a few things sorted first."

"Like what?"

"Like, did Rick say any particulars on that reward?"

"Particulars?"

"I guess what I'm asking is, is this a dead-or-alive situation? In terms of the baby's condition?"

"Condition?"

"I hate it has to be this way, but it's a question needs to be asked."

"You are a piece of freeze-dried shit, Clemens. You are worried about money while a baby has gone missing."

"These are hard times now, Shelton. I'd appreciate it if you spared me your judgment."

"There ain't no reward for a dead baby, Clemens. She's not a fugitive of the law. I'll tell you what, though. Bring me back her dead body and I'll give you a quarter, twenty-five whole cents, right before I shoot you through your skull."

"You'd be a fool to talk to me like that a minute longer," Clemens said.

"How's that?"

"Because I know for a fact Krebs will try to pin this on you when it don't stick to me. Conspiracy to murder, son. You put out the hit."

"I didn't put out any hit."

"According to you, a convicted felon."

"Krebs ain't no choirboy."

"No," Clemens said. "But he didn't beat a man near to death at the Paradise Junction neither. He's not the one deals methamphetamines."

"No," Shelton said. "He deals cocaine."

"Well, you know how it is in the media when it comes to meth. They're biased on it."

"We should figure a way to put this whole thing on Arrow. Fucking Arrow won't mind."

"Either way," Clemens said. "I'm about the best friend you have in this world right now, Potter. You may want to consider them facts before you spout off next time."

"You really think Wolfdog took the baby?"

"I don't know. It was a terrible thought I had and I do believe it should be considered as a possibility."

"We've got to keep looking."

"I'm coming to the farmhouse first," Clemens said. "We need to get a few things straight before I head back out. I need some reassurances. I have already called Rick and left him a message. He has yet to call me back."

"That was a mistake," Shelton said. "You should not have called Rick."

"Well, I did."

"He did not want to be bothered."

"He will be glad to have been bothered when he finds out about Arrow and Portis Dale. I'm on my way over now. We'll sit down in the warm and figure this through."

"I told you I wasn't home."

"I'll meet you there, then," said Clemens.

Shelton hung up, then kissed Kayla's forehead and flipped her back on her stomach. It was her natural position of rest.

Obviously he would not be waiting around to hold some powwow with Clemens. Shelton would go to his nearest trailer instead, to see if he couldn't scrape together a little batch and get himself right.

To be perfectly honest, Shelton needed some meth. He had what they would refer to in the scientific community as a compulsion, though the word didn't quite capture the feeling's significance or strange, sudden power. The way it seemingly arose from nowhere, like a natural disaster or an apocalypse.

Uncle Rick called it jonesing. Well, Shelton was Mr. Jones, stumbling through the barrio. Earlier he was fine, but now he wasn't. To everything there was a season, turn, turn, turn.

Yes, a trip to the trailer would be just the thing. He needed a quiet place to smoke and think through the lies he'd peddle to Uncle Rick before he started spitting them out all willy-nilly. Truth was, he was surprised he hadn't thought to go to the trailer earlier. He blamed the nitrous, which he freely admitted could affect his decision making.

He saw the shotgun leaned in the corner and snagged it for the road. He had finished the pint in the truck and was relieved to find a half bottle of whiskey in the freezer. He grabbed a box of shotgun shells off the top of the fridge, stuffed them in his pocket, and walked back into the cold.

He started the Silverado, then sat inside the idling truck and consulted his whiskey bottle. Shelton enjoyed his nitrous, let there be no doubt, yet there were times you needed a touch of bourbon to go with it, to settle the nerves a little. Nitrous could be reasoned with, so long as you weren't a habitual user. They called it hippie crack, but it could be managed if you knew what you were doing, like Shelton. He had a few slugs from the bottle, felt a blossom of warmth deep in his belly.

He couldn't remember actually putting the truck in gear, but soon found himself driving down the road. He had already crossed Jackson Lake and made it a good ways down Grain and was now nearing the turn for the trailer. It was hard to see in the snow but luckily he trusted his abilities as a winter driver. He knew these hills, too, knew the two-tracks and the trails, the sudden breaks and switchbacks.

Something was bothering him, though, and it had to do with that Glock on the passenger seat. All of a sudden the Glock was making him uneasy. He couldn't say why, but the weapon had crawled right beneath his skin.

Maybe it was because he'd almost killed Little Hector with it, or maybe it had to do with the laser sight and its space-age complexities. It seemed to Shelton that things were complicated enough. What he needed now was the shotgun he had racked behind him. What he needed now was the clear purpose of that long, cold barrel.

He rolled his window down, picked the Glock off the seat, threw it out into the storm, into the howling wind, and felt a quick flush of relief.

"There it is," he said, and turned up the radio.

Guns N' Roses was on and Axl was singing about some girl named Michelle. It was a good song, but Shelton wondered if it was really a girl Axl was warbling about. It seemed a strange time for such a thought, but Shelton couldn't help but wonder if old Axl Rose was a queer. Seemed like he might be, skinny boy like that in leather pants and sang like a girl to begin with.

Shelton couldn't recall if there'd been reports about it or not. Seemed like every few years some rock star turned out homosexual, but Shelton couldn't confirm or deny if that population included Axl Rose. Even if he wasn't an outright queer, Shelton bet he'd tried it. Rock and roll was a life of excesses and experimentation, and it seemed to Shelton that at some point Axl Rose must have held another man's cock in his hands. He probably gave it a few tugs too, just to see what would happen.

"Hollywood nights," said Shelton.

He looked down at the speedometer and realized he was going forty miles an hour. That seemed pretty fast, but then again it didn't.

"It's all relative," he said.

He pushed down on the gas and the truck surged forward. He drank some more of the whiskey down. *Glug, glug, glug.*

He was off Grain Road now but the driving wasn't bad on the little two-track that led to the trailer. It was south of Jackson Lake and west of the river and even with the new snow coming hard through the trees the Silverado's purchase on the trail was solid. His tires were shedding drifts like it was a Chevy Tough commercial.

He gave the gas another punch, a love tap really, then saw a flash of movement on the periphery. A shape hurtling through the blur of snow. It was difficult to see through the window, fogging now in the heat, but he swore it looked like Old Bo was out there running. The window was still down from before and he leaned over and called out for his dog.

The air came in cold and hard and somewhere within that roar of wind Shelton thought he heard Bo holler out for him in return. He squinted into the storm and the less he could see the more certain he became that his dog was out there with him, charging by his side through the blustery night.

He knew Old Bo was dead and gone, yet Shelton swore his spirit was roaming there in the hardwoods. He could feel him, and when he looked out he saw Old Bo restored to his youthful flesh. He saw Bo bound on all fours just like when he was a pup, when he was pure joy and sinewy muscle.

Shelton was just thinking he should slow the truck down, that he didn't want to hit Bo on accident, when he saw the buck charge. He slammed the breaks and the Silverado swung wildly to the left and he gripped the wheel as the truck slid from his control and he watched the big buck pass through the headlights. He saw the high kick of front hooves and the great, cavernous rack. He saw the white of an eye and the wet, spongy nose. Shelton cried out, and he grieved for the animal in the forever that unfolded before impact.

Shelton's front grille met the buck's flank and then the massive body was rolled up into the windshield where Shelton watched the glass explode into a hundred glints of fractured light, shards rising above him as they spun.

Chapter Fifteen

I was still in the trailer, sitting in the room with Jenna, when I saw the headlights. They glared through the hardwoods outside the window. They were two long beams stretching through the dark like planks.

I ran out the back and hurried down the porch steps, thinking they belonged to somebody stuck in a drift. Jenna was asleep in Tanner's blanket and Carletta was still passed out in the bathroom and I thought the driver was likely to have a cell phone and that we would be rescued—but about fifty yards out it occurred to me that whoever was driving was probably Shelton Potter. After all, it was his hellhole of a trailer we were squatting in.

I shut my flashlight off, stooped down, and walked slow and careful. I could hear music, the thump of bass and some screeching guitar, and I moved toward the sound until I saw Shelton's

Silverado angled across a two-track. There was nothing but a few pine trees between us and I dropped to my knees in the snow.

I could see his big, mountainside shoulders slumped over the wheel and the truck's front fender hanging down. The windshield was gone and the cab light was on and snow was blowing in on his motionless body. Twenty yards behind, a buck flopped in the road and I could hear the god-awful wailing through the music and the wind.

There was a felled pine to my left and I crawled behind it and put my chest in the snow. I thought it was possible Shelton was dead and that if he was I could find his cell phone and finally call for help, but he might just be passed out and what if I walked up there and roused him?

All things being even I might have waited him out a little longer, but I did not like Jenna being so far away in the house and I did not like leaving her with Carletta. Her fever had me scared and we needed a phone so I lifted myself into a crouch and eased toward the Silverado.

I got close enough to see the gas cylinder beside his body. The fool had been sucking from a nitrous tank, and there was a bottle of whiskey between his legs that somehow stood unbroken from the crash. Then I saw his cell on the driver's-side floor—a black, blood-splattered rectangle sitting in a pile of glass shards.

I took another step and then Shelton stirred at the wheel and let out a groan. I froze and when he started to bring his shoulders up off the wheel I turned and ran. I leapt for my pine and then made myself small behind it, wriggling as far as I could into the snow and burying my head into my arms.

I heard Shelton whispering to himself, talking hurriedly, and then the clomp of his boots on the snow. I pushed my eyes more tightly closed and held my breath.

I have had nightmares where I realize I am sleeping and try to will myself awake and cannot. In those dreams I am trapped and my last hope is to somehow force myself from my body, to rise above whatever horror is happening and view it from some place that is neither sleep nor being fully awake—but this was not a dream and I could not remove myself from my body but was fully locked inside it instead. I was all cold fear and hammering heart and when I heard the shotgun blast I thought I had been shot until I noticed that the buck's screams were silenced.

I looked up over my pine to see Shelton walking back to the truck. He had the shotgun slung over his shoulder and he was wearing some sort of crash helmet with a black visor and when he turned his head to scan the woods I swear he looked right through me.

I dropped back into the snow and listened to the opening and closing of the truck door. I heard the engine rev and then the Silverado shifted into gear and headed back down the trail.

I watched over the pine until the taillights disappeared into the black and then I stood and ran for the trailer. I ran until my legs caught fire, and when I slipped in the snow I stood quickly and ran harder. I ran and as I neared the trailer I could hear Jenna screaming.

I came in the back. I called out for Jenna and for Mama and then turned toward the sound of the shrieks. The bathroom was locked but I could hear them inside and shook the handle.

"Mama!" I shouted, and pounded the door. "Open up, Mama!"

Carletta mumbled something but I could not make it out over Jenna. I kicked the door and yelled for her to open up, but Mama did not respond.

I ran down the hall toward the bedroom. The light was on and there was a collapsing recliner in the corner of the room where stuffing came through the fabric like cotton bolls. Beside the recliner was a nightstand and on the nightstand was a glass pipe. The papoose had been left but the blanket had gone with Jenna.

Mama would not hurt a baby on purpose, but when she was on a bad one she could slip right into delirium. She could be holding Jenna and squeezing her to death without knowing any different. She could have her pressed to her chest so hard she snapped a rib, or think she was rocking her gently while she was really shaking her out like a rag doll.

There were hangers in the closet, and I took one and untwisted the hook. I looped the papoose over my shoulder and took the straightened wire to the bathroom door. I called out for Mama. I asked her to open up, though I knew she would not. I began to feel for the lever through the pinhead opening in the handle and talked to Jenna through the wall. I told her everything was going to be fine.

"I'm right out here, baby girl," I said.

Jenna screamed and I squatted outside the door and punched with the wire.

"One second, sweet pea," I said. "I'm right here."

The lever finally caught and I opened the door to find Jenna in

Carletta's lap. Mama was sitting in the empty tub, her hair falling across her face in strings and partly shielding Jenna from my view. Carletta rocked back and forth and squeezed Jenna as she wailed.

"Shh," Carletta said. "I'm trying to get this baby to sleep."

"Mama," I said. "It's me."

"I said, *hush*," Carletta said.

"Can I hold the baby for a minute?"

"Tanner is fine right where he is."

"This is Jenna," I said, and lilted my voice hopefully.

I stepped closer and Mama looked up with her gone-away eyes. She looked at some point in the distance, beyond me, and kissed Jenna hard on the forehead.

"He's a good boy," she said. "But he won't stop crying."

"Her name is Jenna," I said.

"He's as sweet as he can be," Mama whispered.

"She's a good baby," I said.

"We've been getting along just fine. I heard him crying and I went to get him and he's finally calming down."

I leaned into the tub but Carletta slapped my hand away and stood. She stumbled as she stepped out but caught her balance and straightened herself against the wall. Jenna reached for me. I reached back but Mama moved into the hall and when Jenna screamed and tried to wriggle free Mama clamped down with her arms and Jenna went still. Jenna's black hair stood on end and I could see the imprint of Mama's sweatshirt on her cheek where the skin was red and puffing.

"Mama, please," I said.

"I've been waiting to see this child long enough," she said. "The boy wants to be with his grandmother for a minute."

I finally grabbed for Mama's shoulder and yelled for her to stop and she wheeled around as Jenna cried out.

"I said we're fine!"

"Just for a minute," I said. "I just want to hold her is all."

Carletta kept her clutch on Jenna and went for the front door, but it only opened an inch before the snow tumbled in and piled on the carpet. I felt the cold push through and Carletta slammed her shoulder into the door but it would not open any further against the weight of the drift.

"Maybe just let me hold her for a minute," I said. "She's probably hungry is all."

Carletta angled toward the kitchen and I knew she was making for the back.

"You and your sister both," she said. "Neither of you trust me with this baby."

"This isn't Tanner," I said.

"You forgot who wiped your asses and burped you in the first place."

"It's okay, Mama. I just want to take her for a second."

"I'm not going to hurt him!"

Jenna jumped when Mama screamed, but then lost her breath in the fright and flushed before she belted out a cry. Mama looked up and her eyes were big as moons and darted.

"I'm not going to hurt this baby," she said.

"I know you're not trying to hurt her," I said. "But can I hold her? Just for a minute? She isn't feeling well."

"He's fine," she said. "The baby is fine."

She opened the back door and stepped out onto the porch. She extended one of her boots and tried to kick the screen door closed but I pushed through it and was careful not to knock her backward.

I held out the papoose.

"Maybe just set her in here for a minute," I said. "Then we can both hold her."

She held Jenna away from her chest now, away from me, and backed toward the steps. Jenna was being dangled over the railing and she kicked her legs and screamed. I could see Mama had no idea at all where she was, that she had no idea that Jenna was in any danger of falling off the deck. Jenna balled her hands into fists and had cried herself silent. Her mouth opened in terrible, silent cries and I reached for her again.

"Mama," I said.

"Out," Carletta said. "Get out of my house this instant, Starr."

"It's Percy, Mama. I'm right here."

"Out! Get the fuck out of my house, Starr!"

Jenna could not catch her breath to scream and I started to worry she might suffocate on her own panic. I wanted to step across Mama to grab her, but I was afraid Mama would jerk away and lose Jenna over the edge. But the longer she stood with her arms stretched the weaker her grip would get, and I worried too that her next step might send them both tumbling.

Mama stood beside the stairs and swayed. Her arms started to shake and finally I came around her side and grabbed a fistful of Jenna's pajamas and pulled. Carletta pulled back and both of us stepped away from the other as Jenna finally wailed and was stretched out between us.

I screamed at Mama. I don't know what I said, but I spit it out like fire. She tightened her hold on the terry cloth and I worked my fingers beneath her fist while Carletta bawled some terrible, animal yelp. Then I set my foot in her thigh and when I kicked her fingers were finally pried loose and she fell.

She did not go down the stairs but only slumped into the snow on the porch where she lay whimpering. I looked down at her and had never felt so disgusted in my life.

Jenna finally gulped air and screamed. She screamed as loudly as I had heard her and I gathered her in close. She shrieked as we stepped back inside and I locked the door behind us and she shrieked as I put her back into the papoose and straightened the blanket over her body. She shrieked while Carletta crawled across the porch, shouting her idle threats into the door.

"You fucking bitch," she yelled. "Open this door this instant! Do you hear me, girl?"

I ran back into the bedroom where I had first found Mama, where Jenna had been sleeping so soundly when I left her in the trailer. I closed my eyes and hummed, but Jenna went right on shrieking. She shrieked while Carletta banged on the back door, and she was still shrieking after the banging stopped.

I was alone in the trailer with Jenna and after a time I looked out the window and saw Carletta wander off into the woods. It was still my instinct to chase after her. Despite everything that had just happened, part of me wanted to try and rescue her again—but I could not leave Jenna and focused on her instead.

I unbuttoned the top of her pajamas and she shrieked louder when my cold hands hit her skin. I fed her a knuckle and she chomped down hard and suckled as I searched her body for wounds. I didn't feel any tears or bleeding but I was not foolish enough to take much comfort in that fact. I knew full well something might have happened inside, though I did not allow myself to dwell too long on what that might have been.

"Baby girl," I said, and stroked her hair.

She worked my knuckle and I wished I had the bottle to offer. I wished I had one more scoop of formula, but that was gone now and there was only the blanket and the papoose and the two of us together in the dark room.

I buttoned her pajamas back up and felt the fever like a flame on her back. I needed to try and cool her down and carried her back to the porch, where I took a scoop of snow from the rail and brought it back inside.

I hated to do it, especially now that there were some stretches of breath between her screams, but I broke the snow up anyway. I put some to her lips and packed the rest to her forehead and stood there and held her through the howling.

I held her until the snow had melted and streaked her face in cold streams and then I dried my hands on my jeans and wiped the water away. I held her close and hard and after a time she finally stilled herself in my arms.

I smiled as I walked her back into the room, but there was no glint of recognition from Jenna. The fever was in her eyes now and she looked back at me without seeing anything at all.

I set her on the carpet and lay down beside her. I hummed

a lullaby, though it was more for myself than Jenna. Jenna was already on her way back to sleep.

I knew I should stay awake to keep watch, to monitor the fever, but I turned in to Jenna and closed my eyes anyway. I held close to her and whispered that everything was going to be fine, though I doubted that it would be. I felt myself drop toward sleep and didn't have the strength to fight it. I was drained of every reserve I had. I was pure empty.

Chapter Sixteen

The drive to the farmhouse was freezing without the windshield, but Shelton could not be bothered by such momentary discomforts, such trivialities. Shelton had just been through a metaphysical experience and for the first time since Jenna went missing he knew exactly what it was he was supposed to do.

Shelton had seen Old Bo's spirit in the woods and it was no coincidence that he had collided with the buck only moments later. What had happened was this: Old Bo had somehow entered the buck, had somehow become the buck as it charged the Silverado. Then Shelton had struck the deer, in effect Old Bo, and killed his best friend all over again.

Shelton knew because he had felt Old Bo's presence as he stood above the buck and watched it writhe in the bloodied snow. He saw Bo's soul itself inside the animal's darting, fear-crazed eye, and when he raised the shotgun to end the gruesome labor of the death he knew that everything that had happened since Bo's passing was not bad luck or unrelated folly.

Jenna's disappearance, his near-catastrophic pursuit of Little Hector, and now the dead buck: all of it stemmed from that one terrible, cowardly betrayal of his faithful companion. Shelton had left his dog to rot like some piece of forgotten meat and that single act would taint everything black until it was put right. What Shelton needed to do now, what he had needed to do all along, was return to the farmhouse and deal with the corpse of his beloved friend.

There was a thump beneath the Silverado's hood as he drove, a rattling in the vents, but everything considered, the truck had come through the collision in fine shape. It had been a good-size buck, an eight-point and heavy for this late in the winter, and Shelton knew he was lucky the truck was running at all.

He crossed Jackson Lake for the farmhouse and remembered the day he'd come home from prison. He'd been nervous about seeing Old Bo, was afraid his best friend, and maybe his only real friend in the world, would begrudge him his absence.

He'd left Bo in the care of Uncle Rick, though care was a term Shelton applied loosely. What Uncle Rick did was come by the farmhouse every now and again, whenever he remembered, and set out some food in a bowl. But he did not take Old Bo out to play, or cuddle with him on the couch and watch football. He did not pet him or scratch behind his ears or tell him that he loved him.

Shelton thought Old Bo might sleep in the living room in protest upon his return from prison, or stalk around the house, punishing him with whimpers and plaintive barks. Shelton wouldn't have blamed Bo if he was vindictive and withholding—Shelton deserved all that and worse—but instead he had come bounding off the porch the second Shelton's tires hit the gravel drive.

Shelton gave the horn three taps, his customary greeting, and Old Bo ran headlong for the Silverado. Old Bo was so excited he ran himself in circles. He jumped and yapped, then ran more circles. He couldn't help it, he was so happy Shelton had finally come home. Imagine that, to be loved so much you turned a friend in actual circles?

Shelton was parked out front of the house now, and for a moment he believed if he wished it hard enough Old Bo would come running through the door one more time. But, of course, Old Bo did not come running.

Shelton was alone. His heart was heavy and swollen with longing and he reached for his tank of nitrous. He did a balloon and then another. He drank some whiskey, gulped it, then reached for another balloon. He did that balloon and then another.

Oddly, the balloons had begun to bother Shelton. It was their celebratory nature, their brightness and whimsy, which he feared had become an insult to Old Bo. The balloons had begun to belie the legitimacy of his grief and finally he just mouthed the nozzle of the nitrous tank and released the valve. *Sssssssssssss.*

He felt the gas hit the back of his throat and explode out his ears and then the brightness opened in his brain like a just-birthed star unfolding.

When Shelton came to, Bob Seger was on the radio singing about being a ramblin', gamblin' man. Bob Seger was born lonely, down by the riverside, where he learned to spin fortune wheels and throw dice.

Shelton understood that he had been unconscious for only a few moments, but that time itself was not definite or linear and that each of those moments held eternities inside their soft, malleable edges and that he had fallen through them somehow and briefly touched forever. He didn't know how he knew that, but he did.

He sat up slowly. Goddamn, he was cold. And where the hell was he? His head hurt, but that wasn't all that unusual and did not concern him as much as the cold. He was sitting inside his truck and he could feel the heat pouring from the vents, yet he was frozen solid. He was shaking like a baby chick. What in the world?

He noticed he was at the farmhouse, and a moment later remembered it was where he lived. But why was it so goddamn cold in the truck?

He reached out with his hand and felt the glassless air in front of him and then recalled the buck and how he'd killed him. Then he remembered that Arrow was dead and that Jenna was gone and that Kayla was inside, hopefully unconscious. He remembered something about Wolfdog taking the baby and how gentle Bo was dead and Shelton had left his carcass in a room to rot.

All these thoughts came to Shelton in a rush and carried with them the initial shock of discovery. It turned out the nitrous had taken him all the way under. He'd uncorked the gas and followed it into some deep, dark cave at the base of his primordial brain, a cool room with stone walls where he'd felt a vast blackness and empty peace, only to come back up and reexperience the horror of each tragic event as it arose in his waking mind. The sadness stunned him and came over him in waves. And then came the regret and the guilt. And finally, the anger. On the radio, Bob Seger had come to the part where the black girls sing. They went, *Ramblin', gamblin' man.*

Shelton stepped out of the truck and his vision was blurred and the hardwoods seemed to spin around him as he walked toward the farmhouse with the shotgun. His steps were heavy and labored in the deep drifts and he could hear his heart beat inside his ears like thunderclaps. He thought maybe he should have taken it easier on the anesthesia.

He was winded by the time he came up the front steps and stopped to lean against the porch rail. His head was throbbing. He wondered if he got worse headaches on account of how big his head was. It stood to reason that he would.

He walked in through the front door and there was Clemens, standing in the kitchen. The funny thing was, Clemens had his hands in Shelton's secret drawer. The drawer where he kept his prerolled joints and the Glock he'd just pitched into the storm. The same drawer where he stuffed his extra cash when he had the good fortune to possess some.

It took Shelton a moment but then he recalled Clemens's continuing role in the evening's drama, how they were to meet back here at the farmhouse to discuss Jenna and the dead bodies. But Shelton couldn't remember Clemens saying anything about rummaging through his secret drawer in the kitchen. It seemed Clemens had gone rogue on that front.

Shelton had walked right in through the front door, yet Clemens hadn't bothered to stop for one minute to say hello. Clemens didn't seem to pay Shelton any mind at all. Clemens was so focused on his effort that he never even bothered to turn around and realize Shelton was standing there with his weapon.

Shelton pumped the shotgun and turned it on Clemens, who finally froze and looked up. His arm was still elbow deep in the drawer.

"I wonder how long you're going to stand there with your fingers in my shit," Shelton said. "Now that the shotty has come into it."

Clemens stepped away from the drawer and put his hands up.

"Now hold on one minute," he said.

Shelton held the gun on Clemens while he bumbled through his ridiculous lies and explanations. He might have even begged, but Shelton couldn't be sure. Shelton didn't hear a single word Clemens said because Shelton was already gone.

Shelton had slipped outside of himself, had left his body so easily and without hesitation that he didn't even notice he was gone until he looked down and saw himself aiming the barrel straight for Clemens's heart. And still he rose. He rose until he reached some place of perfect stillness and symmetry that was both darkness and light, both love and animal rage. And from that distant, blissful remove he watched himself pull the trigger.

The shot hit Clemens at the top of the left shoulder and sprayed the wood paneling behind him. His head snapped back at impact and from the time-stilled heights from which Shelton observed he could see small shards of shoulder bone disperse, like a handful of tiny, gift-store shark teeth, and he could smell the powder and the singed wood as the buckshot burrowed into the wall. Clemens fell back against the kitchen counter and looked up at Shelton with big, scared-shitless eyes.

Shelton had meant to kill him and was both relieved he had not and embarrassed by his poor aim. Here he was, not ten feet away and couldn't hit a man in the chest. Double vision, he supposed.

Clemens pushed himself up off the counter and held up his right hand and pleaded with Shelton as he eased toward the back door.

"Please," he said. "Don't shoot."

Shelton set the shotgun down and leaned it against the kitchen table. He nodded at Clemens.

"All right then," he said.

Then Clemens was gone and Shelton felt himself in dire need of a drink. He walked back to the truck for some whiskey and resolved to stay focused on what was important. Bo. That was what he'd come home for originally, before all this business with Clemens.

He heard an engine turn and looked up and there was Clemens's truck, not ten feet away and stuck in the same little rut Shelton had been parked in earlier. He was just about to walk over and give him a shove when Clemens rolled out on his own and drove off toward the flat black of Jackson Lake. A shoulder shot for attempted robbery seemed about right to Shelton.

"Fair and square," he said. "You old motherfucker."

Shelton had his drink, then capped the whiskey and went back inside. He walked up the stairs and then paused near the top when he heard the screaming. For one hopeful second he thought it was baby Jenna. The sounds were coming from her room and he wondered if after all this time she might have just been hiding somewhere he never bothered to look. Had he even checked the closet?

He ran down the hall but it was only Kayla. She was sitting on the floor with her knees curled to her stomach and the screams were her own. She was clutching a butcher knife from the kitchen and Shelton realized she must have awakened and seen him shoot Clemens. She'd been frightened and gone for the knife, then run upstairs to discover Jenna was gone.

"Kayla," he said, and stepped toward her. "Honey bear."

She screamed again and sat there shaking. Her whole body vibrated like a plucked string, and when Shelton took another step closer she pushed herself along the floor to get away from him. Pushed herself clear across the room. He could see the fear and the animal fury in her eyes and she lifted the knife and held it pointed at him.

"What did you do to her!" she screamed. "What have you done to my baby!"

"I didn't do anything," Shelton said. "I've been out here looking for her."

"You're a fucking liar!"

What he wanted was to sit with her and hold her. He wanted to try and offer some comfort about Jenna, to resolve with her to find the child and somehow repair their ruined lives and start all over again, but Kayla only looked at him and raged.

"You shot Clemens!"

"Baby," he said. "Let's just calm down for a minute and talk."

"You get away from me!" she shouted. "I fucking hate you! I fucking hate you so much!"

Shelton only stood and looked at her. He did not know what to say, suspected that whatever he said would only make things worse.

"Get away from me!" she shouted.

"Okay," he said, and began to back away slowly. "Okay, baby."

He walked out into the hall and then closed the door softly behind him. He listened as she continued to shriek and he understood that she did hate him. She was fucked up, high as she could be, but that didn't change the fact that she believed he had taken Jenna and done the baby harm. And to even think he was capable of such a thing told Shelton all he needed to know. Kayla might have loved him, but she hated him too, and more than anything she was afraid of him. He put his hand against the door and knew in his heart that he would never see her again. In many ways, it was a relief.

He turned toward the other room now, toward Bo. He was through with the distractions and the messing around and he did not bother to cover his nose as he approached the corpse. Rather, he welcomed the stench. He breathed in its black truth and justice because it was exactly what he deserved.

He vomited when he reached the doorway, then staggered toward the body by the dim light of the hall. He stood over Bo and coughed up another mouthful of puke. He cried, as much from the vulgarity of the task as the sadness, then dropped down quickly and scooped the dog into his arms.

Old Bo stunk so bad that Shelton could smell it over the vomit that had come up from the back of his throat and burrowed down at the tops of his nostrils. The flesh hung loose and there were a few buzzing flies, though Shelton guessed the cold had helped some with that particular detail. Still, he could feel how bloated Bo had become and there were troubling bulges in his belly and Shelton feared his fingers might push through the spongy skin at any moment and introduce him directly to whatever horrors of decomposition were taking place inside. It was goddamn macabre, is what it was.

Shelton set the body down on his bed and wrapped Old Bo inside the very blanket he used to curl up and sleep on. There were dozens of black hairs in the fabric and the blanket still held the earthy smell of the living Bo. Shelton carried him to the truck and was greatly comforted by Bo's return to his place of so many peaceful slumbers. It was the first fitting thing that had happened since his passing and Shelton wondered why he hadn't thought to wrap him in the blanket right off.

He set Bo down in the pickup bed and was glad for his missing windshield in the front. It seemed right he should suffer the cold along with Bo. He took a pallet from the stack he kept out by the pole barn and loaded it with a jug of gasoline beside the dog.

He drank his whiskey and as he walked back inside for the shotgun he wondered why Kayla hadn't gone for it instead of the knife. It was puzzling because he'd taught her how to load the shotty himself and she knew how to shoot it.

He remembered that gentle afternoon just a few short weeks prior, the way he'd held his hand around hers and eased them up the barrel and taught her to squeeze the trigger and how he was there behind her to cushion the kick. If she were going to threaten him, he would have preferred she pull the shotgun and do it right. He might have felt a touch of pride then, or at least taken some consolation in the fact that she had remembered that time they had shared and put it to some use.

Instead, she panicked and went for the knife. Well, Shelton thought, it is what it is. She was upstairs behind the door now and likely gone to him forever.

Outside, Shelton got in the truck and drove for Bo's favorite clearing. There was never any doubt about where to put his best friend to rest. Shelton might have squandered every opportunity he'd ever had in this world and been on a run of particularly bad decision making, he might have ruined his life and several others, it was an evolving list, but he was not going to fuck up and put Old Bo to rest anywhere but the wide, brightly lit field where they had so often played together.

A quarter mile from his trailer there was another two-track and it ended in a beautiful little glade where Bo had loved to run wild. On a summer day the sun could sit for hours above that little break in the pines, or so it had seemed, shining on the tall grass and the ironweed while Bo frolicked. While he raced in circles and filled the hills with his buoyant and undimmed barking.

A good game of fetch had always soothed Shelton when he

started to drop his high and tweak and it was doubly nice that the field was right there by his favorite cookhouse. Shelton had always considered it serendipity.

He took the two-track to the clearing, put the Silverado in park, and let it idle. He left his brights on, though they were of little use against the torrent, against the spate of snow and the sky the color of cement behind it. Shelton stepped out the driver's-side door and resolved to complete the work that remained.

He walked the pallet into the clearing first, then came back for the gasoline and whiskey. He drank some whiskey, then set what was left of the bottle in the snow.

There was no way to dig through the frozen ground and give Bo a proper burial, but Shelton believed Old Bo might have preferred it like this anyway. To be set free in a wash of flames, to become ashes and air and be finally and fully released. Shelton thought it was more fitting to the lightness of Bo's spirit than to be confined in the ground, to be buried beneath all that density and dirt. It might not be a beautiful summer afternoon, but it was still their spot and there was sky above them and the space between the pines to find it.

He cradled Bo in the blanket and walked him into the clearing. He set him down on the pallet and pulled the blanket back so Old Bo could see out into the field that one last time.

Now Shelton cried the stinging kind of tears. They were tears of grief, but somehow the hurt was clean and not polluted for once with his own shame and guilt. These tears were strictly for Old Bo, for the loss of his goodness and his brave and loyal heart.

The gas sloshed in the can as he lifted it and the scent cut through the wind and singed his eyes as he uncapped the nozzle and stepped closer to the pallet. He poured the gas over Old Bo and thought it looked a bit like he was seeing him enter the water from above. Like he was standing on some sandy lake floor and watching Bo swim toward him, his face slickened and surprised by the wet.

Shelton turned away and listened to the glug as the last of the gas descended, then heard it splash off the pallet and soak into the snow. Then came the lit matchbook and the flood of heat.

He stepped back from the fire and watched as it all came together, the ashes and the smoke and the snow and the sky, all of it one solid gray slate and the flames beneath it burning. He returned to his whiskey and thought it was probably time to head over to the trailer and cook him up some smoke. It was past time, truth be told. It was goddamn overdue.

He shut the truck off and decided to walk. It was quicker than going back out and coming in on the next trail, which wasn't to mention the near two hundred pounds of buck that was lying dead in the middle of the two-track. No, Shelton figured a little stroll would do him some good anyway, help to clear his mind.

He finished his whiskey, tossed the bottle into the trees, and began his slow amble to the trailer. He watched the shadows from the fire and thought they were like lovely and languid dancers on the snow.

Chapter Seventeen

When I lifted from sleep in the trailer I reached for Jenna, but she
was not there beside me. I blinked my eyes open and when I saw
the empty carpet where she'd been, I felt my heart seize and go
cold in my chest.

Then I heard a voice.

"She's got a fever."

I pushed myself off the floor and turned to see Shelton Potter
sitting with Jenna cradled to his chest. He had his back against
the far wall of the room and I had a dropping sensation, like I was
falling into all that empty space between us.

I wanted to scream but I was too scared. I was too scared even
to move. Shelton had Jenna and I knew that I could not pull her
free, could not wrench her away as I had done with Carletta.

"I guess you're the one who took her, then," he said.

I looked from Shelton to the doorway where his shotgun was

leaned. I doubted I could reach it and wield it in time and knew it would be foolish to try. I nodded.

"I didn't think it would be a girl," he said.

He rocked Jenna and she was so small against his body, like a loaf of bread tucked between his arms. She was not upset, though. She was not crying or trying to wriggle free.

"I love this baby," he said. "I didn't know I did at first. But I know now."

"She's a good girl," I said.

I surprised myself when I spoke and I think it surprised Shelton too. He looked up at me like he had forgotten I was in the room. He cocked his head to the side and held me in his eyes and I felt the fear rise and burn at the base of my throat. Then he returned his gaze to Jenna.

"You're Carletta's girl," he said. "The young one."

"Percy," I said.

"Why'd you take this baby, Percy?"

"She was crying out," I said. "She was right there by the window with the snow blowing in on her and you and Kayla were crashed. I couldn't just leave her there."

"And what were you doing in my house?"

"Looking for Carletta."

"You weren't trying to steal nothing?"

"No," I said. "I am not a thief and I did not drive clear into the north hills in a blizzard to try and steal your drugs."

"No. You just stole this baby."

"I was trying to help her. I am trying to help her."

"I am trying to help her, too," Shelton said. "I've been out here looking for her for I don't know how long. Feels like forever."

"Your boy Arrow was going to gas her. He would have killed her if he hadn't killed himself first."

"Arrow McGraw is not my boy."

"They were coming after Jenna. They said there was reward money."

"There was never any money."

"They were pretty sure there was."

"It don't matter now anyway," Shelton said. "Kayla thinks I took her and blames the whole thing on me."

"She's the mother," I said. "She should not have been passed out like that in the first place."

"I woke up and she was gone. At first I thought she fell out the window and was buried by the snow. I was so sick I thought I would die."

"We're running out of time," I said. "That fever needs to come down."

"I almost shot Little Hector," Shelton said. "Can you believe that? Then I did shoot Clemens. I winged that old fucker and then Kayla came to and could not be reasoned with. That's when I drove out here to put my dog, Old Bo, to rest."

"I could take her to the hospital right now," I said. "I could drive your truck in and get this baby the help it needs."

"I could drive my truck, too," he said. "And take this baby back to her mother."

"Jenna needs a doctor."

"Once them doctors take her, they aren't likely to give her back."

"They shouldn't give her back," I said.

"And why's that?"

"You know why," I said. "She's not safe with Kayla."

"Sounds like you got it all figured out."

"I know what I saw at the farmhouse," I said. "And I know I'm the best fit to help her now."

"Well aren't you high and mighty," he said. "For a tweaker's daughter."

"I'm not nothing," I said.

"Was she crying?" he said. "When you found her?"

"Yes."

"I never even heard her."

"I think she'll be okay," I said. "If I can take her now."

"I didn't mean for this baby to be hurt."

"I know you didn't."

I waited a moment and when he did not respond I inched toward him. I did not want to startle him by standing and slid closer on my butt. I got right up beside him and I could smell the booze and something sharp and metallic on his breath. He sat with his shoulders hunched forward and breathed.

"Everything got sideways," he said. "It all got twisted around."

"You can still make it right."

"It ain't never going to be right. It never was right to begin with."

"You could make it right for this baby."

"Maybe," he said. "Maybe not."

"You can try," I said.

I held out my arms for Jenna and she reached for me as Shelton held her there between us.

"Please," I said.

He looked over at the shotgun and then down at Jenna. I wanted to reach for her but I did not. I sat there and waited and he did not turn to face me but finally lifted Jenna and put her into my arms and she squawked as I slid her into the papoose. I straightened the blanket above her and began to ease away from him.

"I'm so tired," he said.

"You should sit here and rest," I said.

I stood as I neared the door, then stepped into the hall. I was a foot from the shotgun now and knew I could reach it in time if he lunged. I believed I could turn it on him and squeeze the trigger, too—that I would be able to shoot him down right there in the room if he changed his mind.

But Shelton didn't change his mind. He just sat there staring at the floor as I moved into the kitchen. I whispered to Jenna beneath my breath and told her everything was fine, but I knew she would not cry out and startle Shelton. I trusted her completely.

I opened the back door, then eased onto the porch and shut the door behind me. I took a few careful steps to clear the stairs, then bent forward against the wind and ran. The snow fell fast through the pines. The snow kept falling and falling and falling.

I never thought about the keys until I saw them on the driver's-side seat. I was so glad to be out of the trailer I never stopped to realize I'd need the keys to actually drive the truck, and if Shelton wouldn't have left them there I would have just kept running and hoped for the best. There was no way I was going back inside the trailer, and I think it's likely those keys being there on the seat saved Jenna's life. It was the one stroke of luck she'd gotten.

I started the truck and drove down the trail for the main road with Jenna snug in the papoose on my lap. The wind was fierce through the open windshield, but Jenna was beneath it and spared the direct blast. She wasn't crying, and now that we were out of the trailer that quiet scared me. That and her filmy, far-away eyes.

I drove down the two-track until the tires dropped and we hit Grain Road. I put the truck in park then, looked in the rearview and there was nobody coming behind us, at least not that I could see through the snow. I fiddled with the seat lever until I got it to come forward and then I put the truck back into gear and drove.

I nosed for the bottom of the hill and the tires were steady beneath us on the packed snow. The pines and the peaks were dark behind us and the wind was as loud as heaving thunder.

I drove straight to the ER. The hospital is off Highway 31, and the closer we got the more I realized that I was going to have to leave Jenna on her own. That I would have to drop her off and walk away. It was either that or risk all kinds of craziness with the police and social services. I could hear the questions now. *What were you doing in the farmhouse in the first place, Percy? And why did you think your mother was there? What, exactly, was the nature of the relationship between your mother and Shelton Potter? And why didn't you call for help upon finding the baby?*

I was worried the police would pull me on account of the

windshield, but the only vehicle I saw on the highway was a city plow and they didn't pay me any mind.

When I got to the hospital I parked in the far back corner of the lot. I stepped quickly from the truck and did not look down at Jenna. I kept my eyes straight ahead, just like I'd done when we passed Arrow McGraw burning out in the snow. I told myself I was only doing what had to be done. I told myself leaving her was the right thing to do, even as I felt my bottom lip start to quiver.

I set the papoose down just inside the front, sliding doors of the ER entrance. I hit the emergency call button, took one step away from Jenna, and then another. I walked backward until I finally turned and ran into the cluster of vehicles toward the front of the lot. I kneeled down by the rear fender of a van and watched as a nurse ran into the entryway, scooped Jenna in her arms, and then stepped outside to see who'd left her.

Finally, Jenna cried. I felt myself lean toward her, but I did not go back to offer her comfort. I never explained what was happening or said good-bye or that I was sorry that it had to be this way. I just watched the nurse whisk her back inside and felt my heart finally give out and go all to pieces.

I staggered to my feet but held my tears. I knew it was not yet time for me to cry. I was still a mile from our house on Clark Street and the storm was not yet through. I flipped my hoodie up and stepped into the wind. I fisted my hands at my side and I walked.

Chapter Eighteen

Shelton went to the window and watched Percy and the baby run for the truck. He watched them climb in the cab, then saw the headlights hit the clearing and draw back down the trail.

He was glad he'd given Jenna to the girl. It had been the right thing, but Shelton wasn't so foolish as to think it was enough. It wasn't anywhere near enough. What Shelton had done wrong couldn't ever be made right and even the thought of trying exhausted him.

He went for the shotgun in the doorway, then propped the stock in the corner of the room. He leaned over the barrel and wriggled down so that the shot would enter the heart and not leave him as long to suffer.

He reached for the trigger and steadied his stance, balanced the weight on the balls of his feet, and imagined falling into the blast, accepting it without a hesitation or flinch, simply breathing it into his heart so as not to obstruct its passage with doubt or some spasm of muscle, some instinctual, cellular defense against his release.

He breathed in, then out. He closed his eyes and when he fired the load it was not an instrument of justice or redemption, was not an act of self-hatred or of martyrdom, but was only the truth expelled through a smooth-bore barrel, all buckshot and perspicuity.

Shelton heard his blood splatter the walls like a burst of rain on a tin roof, then dropped off the barrel and fell forward. But he was not dead yet. There were still a few remaining thumps of his heart, a breath or two before his last and summative thought, his bitter and tragic final realization.

And it was only this: that so few had ever glimpsed the deepest and most beautiful intentions of his heart.

Chapter Nineteen

I don't know how many days I slept through after everything went down in the north hills. I slept and when I woke I would lay there on the couch, staring out at nothing.

I ate a couple pieces of bread, smoked the few cigarettes I found lying around the house, but mostly kept myself curled up on the couch—clutching Carletta's blanket to my chest as if I were a child.

I had the shades drawn and the days passed in a bit of dim light against the curtains before the night would go black and the cycle reset. And I swear I might have stayed there on the couch until I starved had I not come to and found Deputy Granger sitting in the recliner, hunched over his cell. I sat up startled.

"It's alive," he said, and smiled.

Granger was a friend of my sister's from high school and he was all right for a cop. Whenever I saw him around town he'd say hello and start talking about whatever pictures Starr had posted on Facebook. Which didn't mean I liked him barging in the house or sitting in the living room like he was some sort of governor.

"Can I help you?" I said.

"We need to talk," he said, and cut his phone off.

"Talk about what?"

"For one," he said. "Your sister thinks you're dead. She's on a plane from Portland with Bobby right now. They left the baby with Bobby's aunt and uncle 'cause he has an ear infection and can't fly. Poor little bugger. For two, what the hell was your pickup doing in the north hills?"

Granger was tall and awkward as ever. He had a beak nose and one of those big Adam's apples, looks like a tree knot. He wore a high and tight haircut, too, which only made everything that bulged stick out worse, and I'd bet dollars to donuts he was still a virgin.

"Well, I'm not dead," I said.

"Clearly," he said, and snapped a can of dip in his hand.

Granger is one of those that can't ever sit still. He's all bouncy knees, flinches, and tics, and he worked that tin of Kodiak something serious. *Pop-pop-pop.*

"So what are you doing here?" I said.

"What happened was, Bobby's mother called out to Portland when they released Portis Dale's name on the news. On account of how he looked after you and Starr when you were little."

"Uh-huh."

"Starr tried to call you, but the phone's cut off and you didn't answer any of the five hundred e-mails she sent. Then they had

Bobby's mother drive over here, must have been a half-dozen times, but she couldn't see in and nobody came to the door and your truck wasn't here. She just stood there knocking. Then they called your work and Jeff Pickering hadn't seen you either. You still work out there at the barn?"

"Yeah," I said.

"Well, you might want to call Jeff and let him know you're still alive. He sounded a little worried when I called."

"That's what happens when the police call," I said. "People get worried."

"Either way, Bobby called me and told me they were coming on the plane. He asked me to come out in case something had happened."

Granger finally opened his can of dip. He pinched off a clump between his thumb and finger and when he stuffed it down in his jutted-out bottom lip I could smell it clear across the room. It about singed my nostrils.

"That shit is nasty," I said.

"Then this morning," he said. "We fished out a little Nissan pickup from the hills. Just towed it in and the strange thing is, it's registered to you. You want to tell me anything about that?"

And just like that, he'd gone cop on me. His voice was all, *I'm an officer of the law*, and it ground my nerves something serious.

"Where's my truck?" I said.

"Over there at Power's towing."

"You think you can give me a ride?" I said. "To go and get it?"

"Well, the first thing is how did it get up there? That's the first thing we need to figure out."

"I would guess somebody drove it."

"And who would that be?"

"Who do you think?"

"Typically," he said. "I'm the one that asks the questions in these situations."

"Carletta took it," I said. "I haven't seen that truck in days."

Granger looked at me and massaged the dip with his tongue.

"That's why I haven't been at work," I said. "Which is why I haven't been checking my e-mail."

"You don't let your boss know when you can't make work?"

"Jeff doesn't operate like that. You go when you can and he pays by the piece. And anyway, what am I going to do? Send him a smoke signal? I don't have a phone, man. Like you said."

"So Carletta just drove your truck up to Shelton Potter's and parked it in a snowbank? And you didn't know nothing about it? Not one thing?"

"Man, I haven't seen Carletta in two weeks. You think she leaves little notes around the house when she takes things?"

Granger looked at me for a minute. He made his eyes narrow and hard, like he was in the midst of some serious, detective-type considerations. Finally, he nodded.

"I tried to tell Bobby it was probably nothing," he said. "But your sister had it in her mind something happened."

"Well," I said. "Something did happen. Portis is dead, isn't he?"

And just like that I had reached the limit of Deputy Granger's investigative powers. He spit in his empty Faygo bottle and transitioned to telling me about the county's indigent burial service. He could try to pretend otherwise, but at the end of the day he was a good guy and he wanted to help me. He said once Starr signed some paperwork—I was a minor and of no help there—we'd be able to get Portis a proper funeral.

"They won't be able to put him in the ground just yet," he said. "They'll have to wait until spring to bury him, but you can go ahead and have the service now."

"What do they do with his body?" I said. "In the meantime."

"They basically put him in a warehouse right there on the grounds. Let Mother Nature keep the body cold."

"Jesus," I said.

"It's just what happens," he said.

"Okay," I said. "I guess that would be good. Thank you."

He shrugged and spit again.

"I'll call and leave Bobby a voice message then," he said. "Tell him you're okay. They're due to land in Detroit, but they're canceling flights left and right on account of the storm. I don't think they'll make it up here until tomorrow."

"What storm?" I said.

"I don't know," he said. "The one they had on the Weather Channel this morning. They got their map all covered up in them blue snowflakes. They got reporters live at all the airports in the Midwest. Mass chaos. Good for ratings."

"I'd appreciate it if you would," I said. "I hate that they've been so worried."

"You want to use my phone, call them yourself?"

"No," I said. "Probably better if you do. Make it official."

"Done and done," he said. "Now, let's go get that piece of Jap crap you call a truck."

Granger stood and tucked his hat beneath his arm. He walked across the room all stiff and straight, like cops do, then waited for me at the door.

He hadn't said word one about Mama, which meant her Bonneville hadn't been at Shelton Potter's and that they hadn't seen her when they searched out the north hills. Which meant she was still missing. She was as gone as she was the night I set out for the farmhouse and I had a sick feeling like maybe this time she wasn't coming home at all.

It hit me with Granger right there in the room. A blast of fear that tore a hole straight through my stomach—down in the nervy, low part where sometimes you know things without knowing how.

"Percy," Granger said. "Are you sure you're okay?"

I stood up off the couch and put my hoodie on.

"Compared to what?" I said.

Chapter Twenty

I was at the airport in Pellston the next morning, watching through the terminal window as Starr's little puddle jumper floated in from Detroit. There were five or six other people inside and we were all standing around the giant brown bear mount—Cutler's airport basically being a hunting lodge with airplanes and landing strips.

Everybody was going on about what they were calling "the shootings" and I pretended to ignore them as the plane landed and then rolled to a stop. Starr was the first on the stairs and when she saw me through the glass she came running.

I promised myself I wouldn't cry, but I was bawling as bad as my sister by the time we hugged. And Starr kept on crying. She about soaked my shoulders with tears before she finally let go and wiped at her eyes with her coat sleeves.

"We got to get you a phone that works," she said. "Jesus Christ, Percy."

"I know," I said. "I'm sorry."

"Be sorry while we smoke," she said. "I'm about to die."

Bobby was standing behind her and he hugged me and put me in a little headlock before we followed Starr outside.

There were a few cars scattered in the parking lot and the wind blew and tossed around some corn snow while Starr dug the smokes out of her bag. She hunched her shoulders when she stood and Bobby blocked the wind behind her. She lit up and offered me the cigarette and when I took it she tapped out another for herself.

"I'm sorry you had to fly out," I said. "But I'm glad you're here."

"It's okay," she said. "We would have come for the funeral either way. The bad part is not having Tanner."

"Is he okay?"

"He'll be fine," Starr said. "He's on antibiotics now. We could have brought him in another day."

"I want to see him," I said.

"We'll Skype when we get to Wanda's. She's cooking up a feast for tonight, so you can stay for dinner too."

Wanda was Bobby's mom and she always put out a good spread.

"I'd say bring Mama," she went on. "But I don't really want to see her and I got this funny feeling you don't have any clue where she is."

I looked at my sister but didn't know what to say.

"Shit, Percy," she said. "I never thought she'd stay sober. I've known she fell off since the fall. Or at least I suspected."

"I suspected you suspected," I said.

"I figured as much," she said.

"I should have told you."

"I'm glad you didn't," she said. "I couldn't have done a thing about it anyway, not with a new baby and being all the way out there in Portland. I wanted that time to be with Tanner and not all caught up in Carletta's bullshit. You didn't want to tell me and I didn't want to press you on it. We're even."

We stood there for a moment in the quiet and I looked up at the cloud-chalky sky and let the silence settle. It was the kind of quiet Carletta put between people, and nobody more than Starr and me—a silence full up with everything that couldn't be fixed and didn't need saying again. It was familiar, though, and in that way of some comfort.

"So," I finally said. "How long are you in town?"

The next afternoon we were at the Oakdale Cemetery, out on Clowney Road. Mama still hadn't surfaced and I had the same hollowed-out feeling inside, but I did my best to push it away and focus on Portis. After all, it was his goddamn funeral.

The mortician told us all about the "resting facility" where Portis would be until the thaw and then explained what a nice casket they'd secured for him. He went on and on about how they worked him up like they did all their clients—like we were supposed to throw roses at his feet because he'd done the job the county paid him for—because he'd taken the time to extend basic human decency to someone who couldn't afford it.

There was a preacher at the grave when we got outside and I stood huddled between Starr and Bobby while he said some words. It was cold and there was a low, gray sky. Beyond the clouds was a little reef of blue but I didn't try to see it as some hopeful symbol. Portis was dead. There was nothing that could change that fact and I didn't see the point in pretending otherwise. The snow fell in a mist and the preacher read from his Bible.

I didn't bother to listen to the verse. I didn't care what the preacher said, so long as he was willing to stand there and say something. Portis might have detested religion in life but there was going to be something to his death besides sticking him in a warehouse and walking away.

It was bad enough what they'd done to him on the television. I saw the news the night before, at Wanda's. Bobby's mom had the satellite on and she let it run in the living room while we ate. I tried to ignore it, but I was facing the screen and she played the volume too loud. I was grateful for the meal, but she might have realized that our grief was not being aided by the constant, blaring reminder Portis had been killed.

They kept flashing old mug shots of the deceased and made no distinctions between Portis and the others. The hardboiled journalists at 5&2 News—experienced in the reporting of minor grease fires and advancements in bass fishing technology—said the dead were all "drug users and dealers" and listed their criminal histories below their mugs like baseball statistics.

In a strange turn, which I will not pretend saddened me, the coward Krebs had launched his snowmobile into a pine tree and died just hours after he left Portis to bleed out in the snow. He was probably trying to flee the country, like Portis predicted, or going to ditch the murder weapon he still had in his possession when they found him.

I can't say exactly how I felt when I learned of Shelton Potter's suicide, but I was not surprised. He had looked so far away and alone in that trailer and I think he had already decided how his life would end. I never had to go for the shotgun because Shelton was going to do it himself.

I watched the entirety of that sorry newscast and kept thinking they were going to cut in with a special report on a freshly discovered body. A Jane Doe they'd found slumped over the wheel of a Pontiac Bonneville—but that report never came. The body count remained at four and though anchorman Dick Crutchman never said so out loud, you could tell all along what he was thinking. *There are four dead thugs in the north hills and we are all probably better off for it.*

The preacher didn't waste much time on Portis. The charity package got us about five minutes of his holy ramblings before he slammed his Bible shut and stomped off for the warmth of the funeral parlor. I stared at Portis's snowy patch of grass, there was no marking yet to identify it as his own, and Starr finally took me by the elbow and led me away.

We walked among the rows of graves, a bunch of cement headstones with some names etched in. Sorry plots that were not graced with the lamenting angels and Jesus statues that held court across the highway. In the end, you can't even die your way out of being poor.

I knew it was stupid but it irked me to think of some of those rich bastards, buried in a tomb like King Tut and not half the man Portis Dale turned out to be.

"They got it all wrong in the news," I said. "About that shootout being over drugs."

"How's that?"

"Portis was done with that shit," I said. "He was quit."

"What were they shooting over then?"

"I don't know. But it wasn't crank."

"It doesn't even matter," Starr said. "Either way he's gone."

I turned around to see Bobby trailing behind us. He was looking off at the highway and had his hands stuffed deep in his coat pockets.

"I think it matters," I said, "when they put out a pack of lies about somebody that isn't even here to defend himself."

"It wasn't like Portis was a model citizen."

"Not being one thing doesn't make you another."

"To some people it does," said Starr.

"Exactly," I said. "That's the problem."

"You two were always a lot alike, you know. You and Portis."

"I'm not sure you mean that as a compliment."

"I'm not either," said Starr.

Of course, I could have gone to Deputy Granger and put the story straight. I should have gone to Granger, but I didn't know quite what would happen if I did. Plus, it was so much easier not to. I figured Portis wouldn't have cared either way. Cutler had decided about him years ago, and what good did it do to try and change a bunch of narrow minds now that he'd already gone off to the other side? Portis would want me to keep my head down and go on about my business, at least that's what I told myself once I'd decided it was what I was going to do anyway.

They put out some stories on the news about Jenna, but none of them had to do with how she got to the hospital. None of them mentioned a fever or bothered to touch on her current condition. All they talked about was some emergency hearing and the "safe haven" law. They said Jenna was in temporary foster care, but I'd been there twice myself as a kid and always wound up back with Carletta.

There was nothing on the news about Kayla Hawthorne, about how she was passed out on the floor of that farmhouse while Jenna got snowed on by an open window, and I was starting to worry that everything we went through in the north hills would be for nothing. That Jenna would be delivered right back to where she started.

We dined at the Elias Brothers that night in Portis's honor. I sat beside Starr in the booth and it was good to be beside my sister, to smell her twenty-dollar, cucumber-melon shampoo while Bobby sat across the table with his Detroit Tigers hat pulled low over his eyes.

"He was rough around the edges," Starr said. "But he was all goo in the middle."

"I wish I would have known him better," Bobby said.

"He liked you," I said. "He liked that you and Starr were together. He said he knew your uncle."

Bobby nodded.

"Yeah," he said. "Uncle Karl."

"You remember the aliens?" Starr said, and plunked a handful of fries in some ketchup.

I shook my head and smiled. It was my favorite Portis story of all.

"Of course I remember the aliens," I said.

"This was back when we were all living together," Starr said, and turned to Bobby.

"We were in those old apartments over on Petoskey Street," I said.

"Right," Starr said. "The rat factory."

"They were mice," I said.

"Either way," Starr said. "The point is that they were really nice apartments and we were living there with Portis when he disappeared for two days, which wasn't really a big deal. The thing was, he'd missed work and they'd already called and told Carletta to let him know he was no longer needed. Mama was pissed."

"He'd gone to the arcade," I said.

"That's where he ran into, what was that guy's name?"

"Trout," I said. "I don't know what his actual name was, but everybody called him Trout."

"Right," Starr said. "Fucking Trout. Which is important to the story because he had that misshapen jaw."

By misshapen, Starr meant long as hell. Or, more to the point, troutlike. Plus he had the generally dazed expression of Cutler's prized river fish.

"In the history of the world," I said. "No man has ever looked more like a trout, than Trout himself."

"I think I might have heard of that guy," Bobby said.

"Yeah," said Starr. "He won a Nobel Prize. Anyway, Portis and Trout eventually tired of the arcade and wound up at Paradise Junction. A shocking turn of events. So two days disappear and then Portis shows back up."

"We came in from the grocery store and he was passed out on the couch," I said. "And Mama got right in his shit. 'Where have you been? What have you been doing? Are you aware of the fact that you've been fired?' "

"Never mind the fact that Carletta hadn't worked in months," said Starr.

"Right," I said. "He probably should have pointed that out. But what Portis did was sit up and launch into this story about how him and Trout had been abducted by aliens."

"Honest to fucking God," Starr said. "Aliens!"

"This was when there was a bunch of shows on cable about alien abductions," I said. "Him and Carletta had been watching them and getting all into it."

"So his story," Starr said. "Is all about Trout's jaw, and how the aliens had abducted him to study it. He literally said, 'Trout's jaw has become a subject of intergalactic interest.' "

"That's a direct quote," I said.

"The thing about Portis's stories," Starr said, "is once he got going he started to believe them himself. I mean, he's waving his arms around and giving us all these details about the aliens' eyeballs being oblong and how they could implant thoughts into his head, and how thankfully he had not been anally probed.

"Even in his desperation Portis didn't want anyone to think

he might have been compromised," Starr went on. "That's how deep his homophobia ran. He said, 'I cannot speak for Trout, but I know for a fact that there was nothing ever shoved up my ass at any point.' "

"Wow," said Bobby.

"Classic Portis," said Starr. "Anyway, by the end we were all laughing so hard we forgot to be mad."

I cracked up in the booth. It was good, clean laughter from right beneath the ribs. The kind that feels like a valve releasing. My sister looked at me and exhaled.

"Portis Dale," she said, and shook her head.

"I forgot the part about the probe," I said.

"Are you kidding? That was the best part."

"Unreal," I said.

"I hate these circumstances," Starr said. "But it is so good to see you."

"I know," I said. "It is."

"I don't laugh like this with anyone else."

"Me neither."

"So, I'm going to bring this up now," she said. "Because I don't know when else to do it."

"Uh-oh," I said.

"No uh-oh," Starr said. "Just an idea."

"All right," I said.

"We've got to get back to Portland tomorrow," she said. "I can't stand being away from Tanner and we've both missed too much work as is. I'm going to buy the tickets tonight and I thought you might want to come with us. Just fly out and stay for a while and see if you might like it enough to move."

I pushed some fries around my plate. I knew what she was going to offer before she opened her mouth to say it.

"We've got the guest room," she said. "And Bobby just put in a second bathroom. So that could be yours."

"I even promise not to shit in it," he said.

"That's true," Starr said. "I have him on record there."

"We can cover a plane ticket," he said. "And if you want we can come back in the summer for your little rice burner. We can drive it to Portland, or you could sell it for cash."

"Our district has one of the top high schools in the state," Starr said. "They get all kinds of awards. And the community college is right down the road. It's like two minutes from our house. Bobby and me have already talked about it and agreed to pay for your first few classes if you're interested. I thought I might take one myself. Maybe we could take one together."

"Tell her about the other thing," Bobby said.

"Oh," Starr said, and snapped her fingers. "The college has this great wood shop program."

"Woodworking," Bobby said.

"Woodworking," Starr said. "They run a little store out of the school where they make all their own furniture and sell it cheap. You'd be a shoo-in for that with all the work you've done for Jeff Pickering."

I didn't like Bobby suggesting I sell the pickup, he should have known better than to raise that prospect, but the deal itself was very, very good. I'd have to tell Starr I had dropped out of school, which would be an uncomfortable conversation, but I could get my GED out west and that would probably do—especially if I signed up for some of those college classes in the fall. I was interested in that community college. In that woodworking program.

I sipped from my milk shake and let myself imagine what life might be like in Portland. I thought about how nice it would be to spend a Friday night at the movies with Starr. To be there to watch Tanner grow. To live in a city a million miles from northern Michigan and to have a chance to go to college. To have my own bedroom. My own bathroom, for Christ's sake. I didn't like the rain, but I thought it had to be better than the cold and Starr never stopped talking about how nice the summer was.

I looked at Starr and for a moment I thought I was going to say yes. I thought I was going to say yes and then go ahead and tell her everything else while I was at it. Jenna. Shelton Potter. Carletta in the trailer and how this time I thought she was gone for good. I thought I was going to tell it all, but I didn't. I didn't tell Starr anything because all I could do was sit there and cry.

I cried because I wanted to go to Portland but knew that I could not. I couldn't go to Portland and I definitely couldn't tell Starr why. The second I said I thought Mama was dead she would be on the phone with Granger and more than anything I was not yet ready for Mama to be found. I was not yet ready to trade my fear for the stone hard weight of certainty.

Chapter Twenty-One

I told Starr I'd e-mail her every day, even if I had to drive into work on my day off to do it. Starr said that sounded good, but her heart wasn't in it. She was devastated I wasn't coming and hurried to get into Bobby's truck before she broke down right there in the Elias Brothers parking lot.

"Chin up, kid," Bobby said, and hugged me. "And our offer stands."

Starr and Bobby split town and I tried to stay busy with work. I didn't know what else to do and Jeff was glad to give me the hours.

Pickering's Furniture was just off the highway on one of those dirt roads with no name. The stock was held in the main barn and tagged for sale, but all the work was done in the expansion Jeff built—an insulated workspace he'd had plumbed and heated.

I'd open early and watch the lights flicker on. I'd turn up the heat, brew some coffee, take a fresh pad of sandpaper, and start right in. Mostly I sanded and stripped, but every once in a while Jeff gave me the sprayer and let me cut loose with some lacquer. It was hard work but it paid well and I could set my own hours.

I put in ten-hour days and then I'd drive around to avoid going home. I didn't like the house being empty, but mostly I was afraid of coming up Clark Street to find police cars in the drive. I could picture the neighbors all crowded on their porches, everybody on their phones while the sirens flashed blue and red off the snow. I could see Granger standing there by the door with his hat in hand.

Which wasn't to mention the fact that I still didn't have any idea where Jenna was. I was worried about her, too, and one night I drove over to the Baptist church, thinking her foster family might be the religious type. It was a Wednesday, so I knew there'd be Bible study, and I parked across the street to watch the people file in. I spent a month in foster care in the sixth grade and we went to Freedom Baptist twice a week, including every god-awful Wednesday night, when we'd all sit around tables and take turns reading from the Bible—which was exactly as much fun as it sounds.

I didn't see Jenna, but once I thought I did and even the possibility sent a shiver straight through me. It stirred me up so bad I sat there for another hour just to watch everybody file back out and make sure it wasn't her.

Afterward, I left the church and drove through town. It was as dark and hushed as usual. There was some snow falling through the streetlamps and I saw the orange flicker of a city plow, two blocks up by Penn Park. I wondered what all the downstate and Chicago money was doing now—how were they passing the winter in their bustling and brightly lit cities?

I took another lap through town, smoked my last cigarette, then came home to find the Bonneville had magically reappeared in the drive.

The sight of Mama's car knocked the wind clear from my lungs, but I did not cry. I was too confused to cry. I was angry and I was relieved, but mostly I was shocked. I had been so sure she was gone, but there was the Bonneville and the living room lamp was lit.

I parked along the curb and had a thought like maybe Mama was clean. That she'd been drying out after what happened in the hills and that she'd been gone so long because she finally hit the mysterious bottom they talk about in the movies. The ground zero where great transformations take place.

I had her blanket in the glove. I'd taken it to Portis's funeral to give to Starr, but never did. I kept the blanket for the same reason I didn't tell Starr about anything that had happened, and I took it out now and held it in my hands. If Mama was clean then there would be no better welcome home than the blanket she probably thought she'd lost.

I knew it was foolish, pathetic even, but I folded the blanket in a neat square and stepped from the truck with honest-to-God hope in my heart. A car was coming up Clark Street and I looked down the block at Night Moves while I waited for it to pass. There was blue light from the Open sign above the door and in the dark it cast a glow clear to the curb where somebody stood smoking. It might have been Gentry.

The car rattled by and I hurried across the street and up the front steps. I held the blanket to my chest and looked out at the falling snow. I thought Mama might have heard me and waited to see if she came to the door, but she did not.

Finally, I put my face to the panel window and there she was on the couch—pouring some vodka into a coffee mug and lighting a cigarette. She had some racket on the television, but she wasn't really watching. She was just staring off toward the dark middle of the room. Her knees were bouncing up and down as she knocked some ash off her cigarette and talked to herself, or whoever it was she imagined was with her inside. It might have been me.

I put my hand to the doorknob. It was cold against my palm and I did not turn it. I only held it there and remembered the way Mama had pulled in the trailer and how Jenna had wailed as she was stretched out between us. I remembered how desperate Mama had been and how she crumpled on the steps beneath me when it was over. I remembered how she had called out her pathetic threats.

I looked at Mama but I did not feel that old, familiar anger. I did not feel the rage or the sadness. Even the relief at her return was gone. The only thing I felt now was tired. I was pure exhausted.

I pulled my hand away, turned, and hurried down the porch steps. I ran for the truck, started her back up, and gassed it hard down Clark Street. The sidewalk was empty outside of Night Moves and my tires shot slush as I drove fast through the blue light. I fled Mama the same way I did Shelton Potter—like my life depended on it.

I drove Clark through East Cutler and downtown, but when I came to the highway I did not turn toward the north hills. This time I stopped at the blinking red and headed south. I had no idea at all where I was going, but I drove fast and watched town fade into a soft, distant blur behind me.

I took MacDougal Road off the highway and lost myself on the back roads between Cutler and Porcupine County. In the black sky and gentle snow. I had the radio on country and Emmylou Harris was singing about a wrecking ball. Mama loved that song and as it played I found myself remembering the afternoons she used to take me to feed the swans at Spring Lake.

It was strange. I hadn't thought about those memories in years and all of a sudden there I was, walking into the little lake just off Highway 31. I was only a girl then but I could still feel the warm water and the sand beneath my feet as I waded to the edge of the shallows. I could see the bread crumbs we tossed and how the swans glided straight-necked through the reeds.

Mama had warned me not to, but once I ventured too close. I remembered the hissing and how it frightened me, how it froze me in the water. I remembered the quick jab of a beak, and how I screamed out just as Mama scooped me up and ran me back to shore, laughing.

"I told you, Sweetgirl," she had said.

I remembered Mama straightening my hair after we retreated

to a faraway picnic table, and the way she'd smiled at me in the sun and asked did I want to skip the rest of the bread crumbs and go to McDonald's for an ice cream?

Mama loved me. I knew that she did. She loved me in a way not even Starr could, but it had been a long time, maybe as far back as that day at Spring Lake, that her love had not felt confused and undercut with sadness. This had always been the torment of Mama's love and it remained so now—it was both the sun that had borne me and the endless orbit I tread around its burning.

Emmylou sang and I went along with the words I knew. An angel and a ghost are two different things, but she sounded like both all at once and when she melted into the final chorus it stood my neck hairs on end.

Mama hadn't died. She hadn't even changed. I was the one who'd left her, and that was why I'd felt so torn up and afraid. I made my choice the moment I ripped Jenna from her arms, then cast her into the storm and locked the door against her. All along, I was the one who wasn't coming home.

I drove until I hit the dirt roads and the gravel drives, the far-flung Cutler where trailers sat behind chain-link fence and the yards were strewn with machine parts. I was on the county line now, driving the flatland where it's all cornfields and dairy farms. I passed the giant cross that stood along the edge of the road and then the dirt field where everybody goes to trip acid—where you can see the red pulse of the radio towers, and behind them the blinking lights from the airstrip in Harbor Springs.

The radio played and as one song bled into another there were moments I was certain I could hear Jenna cry. I heard her high-pitched wail, like from when I changed her that first time in the cabin, and though I knew she was somewhere far away, hopefully in the care of good people, my heart still raced at the sound.

I shut the radio off and tried to focus solely on driving but then her crying would come back and I would have to shake my head to clear it. I would have to remind myself where I was and what I was doing. I would have to remind myself that I'd left her at the hospital over a week earlier.

I drove and drove. I drove and smoked cigarettes and by the time dawn broke I could see the snow set around me in high, rolling banks. The sky was like washed metal above the white and I looked out and wondered where Jenna was in all that wide-open space.

I drove until I saw something dart through the fields, something low and black and slanting hard for the truck. I slammed the brakes and fishtailed and I thought I was going to roll until the Nissan settled hard and flung me forward against the wheel. I lost my wind on the impact and then looked up to see Wolfdog standing there in the road. Her front paws were staggered as she leaned forward, her tongue lolling while her breath misted in a cloud.

Chapter Twenty-Two

This was how I came to leave Cutler. I left Mama at the house, found Wolfdog, and knew it was time. I knew it was past time.

I pushed the passenger door open, called for Wolfdog, and she trotted over and jumped in the cab. I put my hand out to pet her and she sighed and leaned in for a nuzzle.

"Hey girl," I said.

She barked brightly and I put the truck in drive. I could smell the funky heat of her breath and her head was enormous right there beside me. Her face was flat beneath her straight-standing ears and her jaw was sharply angled until it disappeared into the snout. Her pupils were black and rimmed pale blue and there was a welcome in her eyes that just about tore me down.

We drove back for the highway, then through town. I stopped for gas and to get Wolfdog some food and it was full sunup by the time I parked across the street from Granger's little house on Poplar Street.

He had a small square of a yard and a basketball hoop on the garage where the rim sat buried in snow. I could see him inside through the kitchen window, sitting at the table and picking through the paper. He was drinking coffee and looked up every so often to glance in the direction of the television—a big flat-screen I saw flickering through the living room curtains.

Wolfdog sat in the cab and twitched her ears. Then she shook out her fur and barked.

"All right," I said. "I'm going."

Granger came to the door in a Sheriff's Department T-shirt and gray sweatpants and he flinched a little when he saw it was me. Maybe he was expecting the Mormons.

"Well, this is a surprise," he said.

"I come in peace," I said.

"Jesus Christ," he said, and nodded at the truck. "Is that Portis's beast out there in the cab?"

"Her name's Wolfdog."

"The truth be known," he said. "She's always looked more wolf than dog to me."

"It varies," I said.

"Well," he said. "How about a cup of coffee then?"

Granger's wheels started turning right away. I asked if he knew anything about the baby they'd been talking about on the news and he shot me a look—his brow all narrow and staggered while he leaned against the kitchen counter. Then I saw the light come on, watched it bloom into a little half smile as he shook his head. He came to the table with the coffeepot, poured me a cup, and topped off his own.

"What brought about this interest?" he said.

"Just a concerned citizen," I said.

"Very concerned," he said. "It would seem."

He returned the coffee and then settled into his chair. He aimed the remote, shut the television off, and pushed his newspaper aside. He started packing a tin of chew.

"It's just that I'd be curious to know how she was," I said.

"Is that right?"

"I guess what I'm wondering," I said. "Is what happened to her afterward. You know, after she was left?"

He nodded, then scooped out a dip and tucked it in his lower lip.

"What I'm wondering," he said, and jabbed down the dip with his tongue. "Is if whoever brought that baby in might also know something about what happened in the hills with all them dead bodies?"

"I don't know," I said. "If you ever find them, you should ask."

"Nobody's looking," he said. "That's the thing. Michigan's got a safe haven law—means if you have a baby in harm's way, you can bring them in, drop them off, and not answer a goddamn question about anything. Legally you have every right to turn around and walk away. Case closed. They passed that law to try and keep babies out of Dumpsters."

"It sounds like a good law then," I said.

He shrugged.

"I don't know if it is or it isn't," he said. "It's just the law."

"That safe haven thing probably doesn't apply to dead bodies, though, does it?"

"No," he said. "It does not."

Granger leaned down and picked up an empty bottle of Faygo cola he must have had sitting on the floor by his chair. He spat and then set the bottle back down by his feet. Polite.

"So this baby," I said.

"Right," he said. "Because you were sort of wondering, as a concerned citizen."

"Yes," I said. "Exactly."

"It's pretty simple really," he said. "The hospital called us after the drop-off and treated the baby. Then we called the judge. Judge shut off the Michigan State game, called an emergency hearing, and came down to the courthouse. Standard operating procedure. Judge ruled the baby be placed in temporary foster care until the adjudication and turned it over to Family Services."

"Adjudication?"

"It's basically like a trial. They just call it something different."

"When's that?"

"Has to happen within sixty days."

"What about the mother?"

"Kayla Hawthorne? They found her wandering around the north hills when the storm cleared. She was high as hell and hysterical. Woke up to find her baby gone and took off to find her on foot. She was clutching a butcher knife for some fucking reason."

Granger looked at me and must have noticed my surprise. I

couldn't believe he was telling me what he was, that he was calling people by their names and dealing in specifics.

"Everything I'm telling you right now," he said. "Is public record. You can walk right down to the courthouse and ask to see the file."

"Is that right?" I said.

"That's right," he said.

"So where's Kayla Hawthorne now? Is she in jail?"

"Jail?" he said. "Hell no, she's not in jail. They don't put you in jail for being a shit mother and a drug addict. She's wherever she usually is, doing whatever it is she usually does."

"So what's going to happen at the trial?"

"They're going to take the baby away and she'll probably be adopted by the foster family that has her now. Kayla could fight it, but she's already lost one and it would be a long shot. Then again, she might not even want to try and keep it. If she doesn't, she can call the court and they'll be over in zip-point-shit with the paperwork. Family Services wants that baby out of the home. That much I can tell you for sure."

"That's good," I said.

"Yeah," he said. "It is good."

"And the baby's okay?"

"She had a hell of a fever, but it come down. She's got a clean bill of health, far as I know."

"And what about the father?"

"What about him?" Granger said. "Your guess is as good as mine. Good as Kayla's probably. Now, can I ask you something?"

"Sure," I said.

"What are you going to do? After all this mess?"

"Portland," I said. "I think I'm going to Portland."

"Really?"

"Yeah," I said. "To move in with Starr."

"As long as you're not running off with some dipshit you met on the Internet."

"As you know," I said. "I don't have the Internet."

"You taking the truck?"

"Yeah," I said. "And Wolfdog."

"I won't worry about you out on the highway then," he said. "Not with her riding shotgun. Just don't get pulled. I assume she isn't registered."

"I won't get pulled," I said.

"I got some gift certificates," he said. "Meal deals at BK, if you want to take them for the road. I got a whole stack over there clipped to the fridge."

"You trying to get rid of me or something?"

"No," he said. "It's just that you got to get out while you can. This place has a way of sucking you in if you let it. Like quicksand."

"I won't let it," I said.

"Good," he said. "Then take the damn gift certificates."

"Thank you," I said. "Thank you for helping with Portis and for everything else."

"Protect and serve," he said. "You know how it is."

"Granger," I said. "I do have one more favor to ask. If you wouldn't mind."

Chapter Twenty-Three

The foster parents were Matthew and Rebecca Farmer. Granger
didn't know them personally, but had heard they were good
people. That they'd been on the wait list for some time and were
thrilled when the court called about Jenna.

He scratched out their names and address and I was glad to
see it was on Williams Street in West Cutler. It was all oak trees
and wide sidewalks over there—a nice neighborhood with a
Montessori school and beautiful old homes—none of that tacky
new construction like you see along the water.

Granger left for work and told me to crash out on the couch
for a while if I wanted. He said I looked tired and that I should
get some rest before I drove clear across the country. I told him
I would, but sat at the kitchen table instead and wrote out my
letter.

Granger had notebook paper and some envelopes right there

on the kitchen counter and I was resolved to tell the Farmers everything. Everything I believed they needed to know.

I refilled my coffee and I wrote. I described finding Jenna by the window and the way the snow was slanting in. I told about the pickup being buried and walking along the river with Portis. Then we'd hiked to the shanty and tried to drive out and when we couldn't Portis had died trying to save me and Jenna both.

I left out the part about Carletta in the trailer. I didn't see what good it would do anybody to know what Mama had done, so I kept my focus on Jenna and how strong she had been. How incredibly brave she was. I wrote about the papoose and the blanket and how we'd fed Jenna on formula and melted snow. I told about Shelton Potter in the trailer and how he'd done the right thing and let me take Jenna. I could not say that he was a good man, but I could say Shelton Potter was more than the bad things that he had done.

It came as a surprise to me, but it felt good to put it all down. To tell my story and see it in black and white. To see it on the page and as something outside of myself. I felt lighter for the truths I'd told, but saw no profit in revealing who I was.

I'm the one who found her, but I'm not the same person I was before. I am different now because of Jenna and Portis Dale and I believe we all tried to save each other in that storm and that mostly we did. I know Portis came to love Jenna in that short time and that he was changed by it.

I included a brief postscript that explained, among other things, that the Farmers should not try to locate me.

I will be somewhere else. And if anybody comes to you with a story that disputes the events described in this letter they are an outright liar and not to be trusted. If you need proof of my account I can tell you about the terrible rash Jenna had beneath her diaper and that she was bone skinny and in possession of two little nubs of teeth at the time of these events. I'm sure the doctors/police took pictures if you feel it necessary to validate my claims.

I sealed the letter in the envelope, then grabbed an empty grocery bag Granger had in his pantry and took everything out to the truck. Wolfdog sat up and barked and I hurried toward her. I opened the passenger door to pet her and told her everything was all right. Then I took Carletta's blanket from the glove and dropped it in the grocery bag with the letter.

Mama might have intended the blanket for Tanner, but it was Jenna who'd been swaddled in it. The blanket had helped to carry her and keep her warm in the north hills and that made it hers.

I drove down Poplar Street with Wolfdog beside me in the cab. I'd stop at Pickering's on the way out of town for my last paycheck and there would be enough for gas, and even some food if we got tired of Burger King. We were going to make it to Portland, there wasn't a doubt in my mind about that.

We took Poplar to the highway, past the cement plant and the trailer park, and then made the turn for town. We drove by the Methodist church and City Hall and I watched the sun glint off the waterfront where the waves were frozen in mid-tumble along the shore. Beyond the shore was the bay and I could see the slow push of a freighter in the distance where the ice broke into blue water and ran clear into sky.

I turned into West Cutler, then onto Williams Street, where I slowed as I passed Jenna's new home. I think it was what they call a bungalow. One of those cute, California-looking houses, and sharply painted to boot—everything forest green and trimmed orange. I drove to the end of the block, then looped back and parked across the street.

The Farmers had their sidewalks shoveled and a trimmed hedge that lined their drive like a fence. There was a big front porch swing, bird feeders staked throughout the yard, and a brightly colored sign above the door that said WELCOME.

There was a red Pontiac Vibe easing slowly toward us on the street, and then the left blinker came on and it turned into the Farmers' drive. My first thought was to put the truck in gear and drive away, but I did not.

I watched Mrs. Farmer get out and I put her somewhere in her mid-thirties. She had beautiful red hair that fell down around her shoulders and wore a yellow North Face jacket and blue jeans. And when she lifted Jenna from the car seat I felt my breath catch.

Jenna called out in that sweet, high-pitched babble and Mrs. Farmer smiled as she swung her onto a hip. Mrs. Farmer reached back into the backseat for a bag of groceries and then bounded up the porch steps while I sat there watching with a cave in my chest. They both looked so happy.

I didn't know what I was going to do now, had never planned that they might be home. Wolfdog's side ballooned with easy breaths, though, and that calmed me as I waited a few moments and then stepped out of the truck.

I held the bag against my side and jogged up the drive. I could see more groceries in the hatchback and hurried up the porch steps. My mouth had gone to cotton and my breath was quick and short in my lungs.

The front door was open and I could hear music playing softly from the back of the house, maybe from the kitchen, and when I went to set the bag down I looked through the screen door and saw Jenna on a play mat inside.

She was on her back and batting at a stuffed animal that dangled above her. She was in a small room to the side of the entry and between her and the door was a long hall that led straight to the back of the house.

I watched her and remembered the bassinet and the way she'd screamed out against the wind. I remembered carrying her through the snow and how Portis had helped me when she grew heavy. I remembered her sleeping beside me in the shanty and the way she chomped my knuckle for comfort when she'd finally been freed from Carletta. I remembered Shelton placing her in the papoose and how the snow still fell as I ran for his truck.

I watched her now, in a long-sleeve onesie with sewn feet and her black hair shooting off in all directions. She cooed as she played and when she turned toward me I swear her eyes widened into saucers and were all shot through with light. Jenna went *gheew* and parted her lips into a smile. She reached up a hand and I put my palm against the screen.

I saw light through the double-hung windows in the living

room and could make out the music from the kitchen more clearly now. I heard the sound of acoustic strumming and the clank of cans as Mrs. Farmer put up food in the pantry. I could hear the chatter of children playing in a neighboring yard and the faraway rumble of a truck on the highway.

I said, "Good-bye, Sweetgirl."

TRAVIS MULHAUSER is from Petoskey, Michigan. He currently lives in Durham, North Carolina, with his wife and two children.